SWITCHBLADE HEART

SWITCHBLADE HEART

Denning

ARCHWAY
PUBLISHING

Archway Publishing books may be ordered
through booksellers or by contacting:

Archway Publishing
1663 Liberty Drive
Bloomington, IN 47403
www.archwaypublishing.com
1 (888) 242-5904

ISBN: 978-1-4808-1881-1 (sc)
ISBN: 978-1-4808-1882-8 (e)

Library of Congress Control Number: 2015908285

Print information available on the last page.

Archway Publishing rev. date: 7/24/2015

This novel is dedicated to Norman, who fought bravely, and Adrienne who loves fiercely.

July 1, 1986, 7:29 P.M.

"Accidents happen in my line of work."

Roland's face contorts in a mix of fear and anger an instant before the car hits me. Some instinct pushes me toward the sidewalk, but too late. I'm flung into the street like a piñata. A surprised, pissed-off piñata who swallowed her gum and bit her tongue.

"Hey! You asshole!" Roland shouts at the car as it speeds off. He runs to my side. "Reno, you okay?"

I'm fine, but the car knocked the wind out of me and I can't answer. I nod as I struggle to force air into my lungs. Although I only got a glimpse of the driver's face, I'm pretty sure it was one of Zhukov's men. All of those fucking Russians specialize in the same stupid dismissive arrogance, especially toward women. But why try to kill me in particular? Maybe just professional opportunism? Or maybe he's just a dick. Probably both.

"Don't move," Roland says. "Something could have ruptured or broken. I'll bring the car around and get you to the ER."

I want to protest that it's just a glancing blow, no need for a doctor. But he's already gone and I realize that I've been sitting on the curb for a while now. Maybe a concussion? Roland drives up and helps me into the backseat, where I gaze at the upholstery for a moment before passing out.

Roland hits the first speed bump near the hospital a little hard, bouncing me off the backseat. I sit up, feeling a bit woozy but not too bad.

"Sorry," Roland says.

"Hey, I feel okay. Let's just skip the whole hospital thing."

But he won't be dissuaded. Fifteen minutes later, we're in a tiny exam room.

"Doctors always make you wait," I say to Roland.

Slouched in a small vinyl chair, Roland cracks his knuckles, his old fighter scars flashing in the fluorescent light. "It establishes authority and hierarchy."

I puff air from my cheeks. "I'm going to make Zhukov pay."

"Somebody'll probably do it for you. I don't think he has many friends. Besides, he mostly missed you. Could be a lot worse."

I twist my neck over my shoulder and try to gauge the severity of the mottled bruise spreading down my side. It could be worse. I could be dead. So yeah, could be a lot worse.

"Modesty check," coughs Roland.

I pull up the idiotic paper gown that hospitals always make you wear and glare at Roland. "Pervert."

"Flasher."

"I'm going to shoot Zhukov."

Roland yawns. "You already said that. And you don't know he was responsible."

"It was him. And he's not getting another chance."

"You can't always be Missy Badass," he snorts. "You

should adopt a new outlook. You know, find peace and serenity within yourself."

"Screw you."

Roland closes his eyes and sighs. "This is what I'm talking about. Your attitude doesn't invite serenity. It kicks serenity in the nuts. And serenity doesn't like getting kicked in the nuts."

I laugh. Roland always makes me laugh. "Next chance I get, I'll give serenity a blowjob. Happy?"

Roland balls his hands into big fists. "Not really. I could use some Percs…" He opens a scarred eyelid and peers at me. "You think you could convince the doctor to give you something?"

"You should stay away from that shit. No good for you."

He grimaces and flexes his hands again. "They ache."

"Quit punching people."

"That's my job."

"Let's get out of here," I say. "I don't want to be late for Victor." My boss hates it when we're late. I slide off the table. The cold tiles kiss my bare feet and send a shiver through my body.

"Just stay put, sunshine. I'll find out what's taking so long."

Before I can reply, the door swings open. A doctor enters the room with a chart under one hand. Squinting through a pair of thick glasses, he peers at the chart. "Reynosa Villarrubia?"

"Call me Reno," I say, reluctantly sitting back down on the table.

He nods. "I'm Dr. Barrington. Sorry to have kept you waiting. The labs are running a little behind today." He squints briefly at Roland and then gently runs his hand along my spine. His hands are warm and soft. They feel nice, like he actually cares. And he might. He seems like a guy who would care. "It looks like you had a bit of an accident, hmm?"

"Yeah, something like that." I smell mint on his breath. Baby fat still rounds his jaw. He looks like he doesn't even shave yet.

Barrington hums to himself as he presses and pulls on my shoulder, occasionally inquiring whether I feel any sharp pain. "While your shoulder suffers from some deep bruising, it should heal without any complications," he says. He adjusts his glasses and adds, "But we have other matters to discuss."

I frown, raise my arm, and stretch. "Like you said, Doc, it feels a little sore but not broken." I take a deep breath and no pain flares.

Barrington turns to Roland. "I need to talk with Miss Villarrubia privately." He gestures to the door. "Do you mind?"

Roland gives me a bemused look. "Don't hide the pain, *Miss Villarrubia*. Not good for you. I'll call Victor, let him know we'll be a little late." He stands up with a wince. "Get something so you can sleep," he adds before sauntering out of the room.

Barrington closes the door behind him and removes the x-rays from the envelope. He slaps them onto a light panel on the wall and turns off the overhead light. The ghostly luminescence of my bones fill the room.

Eyes hollow and dark in the dim light, he faces me. "Your x-rays show a pattern of abuse and injury. I can see numerous signs of old fractures." In a gentle, sweet tone that makes me like him even more he says, "It's just a matter of time before something serious happens again."

I shiver in the cool air and hug my paper gown. "Accidents happen in my line of work."

"What your boyfriend is doing to you is wrong. You're not to blame. There are people who can help you."

"What are you talking about?"

"You survived this time, but in most cases domestic abuse eventually leads to injuries serious enough to cripple or even kill." He removes a business card from his coat pocket and extends it to me. "Please call the number on this card. They will provide you safe shelter and counseling."

I finally understand. "Doc, nobody's beating me and I'm not dating anybody." I jerk a thumb in the direction of the door. "Especially not that guy." I pick up my blouse and begin to squirm into it beneath the gown.

Dr. Barrington holds up his hand. "I need to report this." His eyes abruptly shoot to the ceiling as I give up using the gown as cover and just rip the shitty little thing off and throw it to the floor. Patience is not one of my virtues. I'm barely on speaking terms with polite or classy.

"At least take the card in case you change your mind."

I ignore the card and pull on my jeans. "I'll try to be more careful." But I can't help glancing at the x-ray. The splintered webbing of healed fractures are stark white against the pale gray, reminders that I hadn't been careful enough in the past. Just as I hadn't been tonight…

As I finish dressing, I try to ease the pained expression on Barrington's round, soft face. "It's not domestic abuse, Doc. And I can take care of myself." I push by him and let the door close behind me.

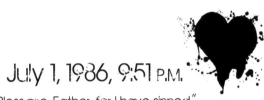

July 1, 1986, 9:51 P.M.

"Bless me, Father, for I have sinned."

Roland eases the sedan out of the hospital parking lot and drives toward the edge of town. I hate to be late, especially to meet Victor. Waste of time with that doctor. Pretty sure Roland only took me because he wanted some narcotics. I shake my head, annoyed at us both. Two steps behind the whole day.

"I still can't believe he said that," I say to Roland.

"Domestic abuse is more common than you think," he replies.

"Not that," I laugh. "The thought that I would actually be dating you."

"You're fucking hilarious. *I'm* the one who should be insulted. I'm surprised he didn't peg you for a lesbian with your all-you-men-can-go-fuck-yourself-with-a-broomstick attitude." He cracks his neck and flares his nostrils at me.

"I don't hate all men, just some. Those Russian bastards especially."

"You need a man."

"So do you."

"I'm serious. Everybody needs somebody. You can't deny

the body. You can't lie to your heart and you can't fool your pussy. What about Jack? He's interested."

In no mood to hear Roland's lecture on my love life—or lack thereof—I roll down my window and let the wind drown him out. But he's right. For a complete jackass, he's right a lot.

But Roland won't leave it alone. "Jack's a good guy," he yells over the roar of the wind. "You should encourage him a little, you know?"

"I'm not good at encouraging," I yell back. In fact, I'm not good at anything with men unless you count creating awkward silences and punctuating them with sarcasm. I'm like that with people in general. Everyone else seems happy and carefree and somehow optimistic that everything is going to work out and everyone loves them. I'm the girl who gets hit by cars, carries a switchblade in her boot, and has killed more men than she's kissed.

In twenty minutes, we reach Victor's estate. Roland rolls to a stop in front of the iron gate, black and pitted with age, that encircles the property. He punches a code into a discreet touchpad near the intercom, and the gate ponderously swings open.

Roland drives the sedan up the gravel driveway, the tires crushing into the stones like grinding teeth. The stars dim as clouds slide over them. Rain tonight probably.

Victor exits the house and trudges toward the car. He waddles over to me, leans through the window, and kisses me on the cheek. "What did the doctor say?"

"Just a bruise," I say. "It's nothing."

Victor smiles, his fleshy face creasing into rolls. He opens the car door and the backseat sighs as it receives his weight.

"Roland, did Reno thank you for saving her life?" he asks through the privacy partition.

"Not exactly," Roland replies. "I think she's too busy planning Zhukov's funeral. Oh, but she did find the time to report me for domestic abuse."

Victor clucks his tongue. "Leave Zhukov to me, Reno. I'll talk to Gartello. But I think you should thank Roland."

I roll my eyes. "I already thanked him."

"No, you didn't," Roland says.

"To the church, Roland. We're already late," commands Victor.

Roland pulls out of the driveway as a light rain begins to speckle the windshield. We pick up speed and head downtown. The streetlights twinkle on the raindrops as they plink against the glass.

We arrive at the church as lightning flares in the underbelly of the clouds drifting over the city. The wind gusts, swirling my hair around my face as I climb the back steps of the church. Victor follows me and Roland forms a rear escort, his eyes mostly scanning the street for any approaching vehicles that could pose a threat.

I leave Victor waiting just within the doorway with Roland while I stalk the pews. My gun glints in the wan light of the prayer candles. I sweep each row, not expecting anyone but still cautious.

I remind myself to look at the hands first. When startled, most people look at the face, but the face never holds the danger. Any blade or gun lives in the hands.

I check the confessionals last. I creep up and jerk the door open. Father Ramirez whirls toward me, his mouth opened in a round O of surprise. His thin, pinched face always strikes me as more of a scholar's than a priest's. I flash him a grin and then slam the door shut, briefly irritated with myself for looking at his face first. I check the other confessional. Empty. Satisfied that no homicidal assassin is lurking in the church, I nod at Roland, who locks the back door and escorts Victor inside.

I watch Victor shuffle over to the confessional booth and squeeze his bulky frame through the doorway. As the door shuts, I overhear him say in his sonorous voice, "Bless me, Father, for I have sinned."

I wait with Roland a few steps from the confessional near a statue of Mother Mary. Roland lights a cigarette from a prayer candle, his face momentarily framed by a warm golden glow. He looks almost like an angel, if an angel looked like a giant in a gorilla suit. He takes a drag and steps back into the shadows with me.

"Hey, remember that guy I shot last week?" he asks, smoke from his cigarette curling around Mother Mary's face.

Not this again. "Which one?"

"The guy who sparked. Remember him? I finally figured it out. The bullet must have hit his fillings." He smiles like a big kid. "What a shot."

I scowl at him. "Don't talk about dead guys here. And put out that cigarette."

"Why? Victor smokes in here."

I shake my head. "It's wrong. And you're not Victor. Put it out."

He throws it away. The glowing tip pinwheels into the darkness and bounces at Mother Mary's feet. The smoke lingers in the cool air. "You scare the shit out of a priest with a gun and yet smoking is forbidden?"

"Gun is part of the job," I say with a shrug. "Smoking is just a bad habit."

The moon slips free from its shroud of clouds and glimmers through the stained glass like a frozen opal. I wonder who built this church. What induced them to depict the saints in such tragic poses, arms stretched in agony and faces appealing to Heaven? Trapped forever in the glass above me, rimmed by the moonlight, the saints definitely suffer more than the sinners.

Roland nudges me. "Reno? Did you hear me?"

"Huh? Oh, sorry. What?"

"You sure you're okay?" he asks, peering at me. "We still meeting with Carter tonight?"

"Yeah, guess so."

"If you really want to shoot somebody, he would be my choice." Roland holds up a big meaty fist, the scar tissue ridged and bunched around his knuckles. "I'd like nothing better than to feel his face crack open."

"Who needs work on his serenity now?"

"We'd all be better off if he disappeared," Roland says softly. "No matter what Victor says."

"Nothing you can do." I gesture to the back door and wave him away. "Cover the exit and I'll take the confessional."

"You always take the confessional."

I shoo him toward the door. "Too bad."

He smirks. "Isn't eavesdropping some sort of sin?"

"Mind your own business."

"You first. Eavesdropping only causes heartache." But he ambles to the opposite corner, blending into the shadows, and watches the door for unwelcome visitors.

Once Roland is in position I ease over to the confessional

and press my ear to the wooden wall. If it's a sin to eavesdrop, I'm definitely going to Hell. But I'm probably going to Hell anyway for a bunch of other things. Victor too. I strain to hear him talk to Father Ramirez.

"Split the money like before—equal parts in the orphanage, church, and consulates," Victor says.

There's a long pause.

"And something for you, of course," Victor adds.

Father Ramirez gets pissed like always. "Nothing for myself, Victor. You know that."

I hear the confessional bench creak under Victor's weight. "I encountered difficulties."

"You say that every week."

"Divesting myself of my types of business might be impossible," Victor grumbles. "My attempts to negotiate are perceived as weakness by my enemies, and they redouble their efforts."

"Every act of hate and sin only narrows your options further," Father Ramirez says in a weary voice. "Just leave. Take what you can and find a place where you can start fresh."

"I've lived here all my life. All the people whom I respect and love live with me in this city. Leaving here would be like leaving my life. But it's different now. My old friends, people I trusted, are being replaced by predators with no honor or history." After a brief silence, Victor's voice brightens. "The sponsorship documents arrived yesterday. Maria Gonzales got her green card."

I press my ear harder against the side of the confessional, trying to hear better.

"You can't trade with God, Victor. Helping the innocent doesn't make you one of them."

I hear Victor shift his weight in the small booth. "I don't presume to barter for my soul, Father. But you'll be happy to know that I'll be completely free of my burdensome partnership with Carter Hansen in just twenty-two days. Many of my difficulties will evaporate with his departure. Until then, I do what I must."

Twenty-two days and then no more Carter? I smile in the darkness at the thought of life without that jackal. This is the best news I've heard—well, overheard—in a long while.

"Twenty-two days will turn into twenty-two years," Ramirez sighs. "If you won't leave, you can at least stop initiating the violence. And don't react to their invitations to sin."

"I have little choice," Victor says in a sharper voice. "Not everyone makes the world a better place, Father. Many of my adversaries are vermin. They were all due for an ugly fate sooner or later. I just make it sooner."

"That's God's job, Victor, not yours," Ramirez says gravely, like he always does.

Victor grunts something that I can't follow. Whatever it was must not have satisfied Father Ramirez.

"Victor, I want to help you," the priest snaps, even more irritated than usual. "But if you don't renounce your current life, it will eventually consume you. There's nothing you or I can do to prevent that. It's the nature of your path. You must find another way."

I hear Victor rise. I dart away just before he bangs the door open and steps out. The shifting air swirls the candle vapor and incense around me.

"We're done here," Victor says without looking at me.

Roland unlocks the back door as we approach. An

ambush seems unlikely since few people know of Victor's spiritual habits. I think his enemies would be surprised that God didn't strike him dead the instant he set foot inside the church.

It didn't seem sinful to listen to Victor piss off Father Ramirez. As his sins invariably entwined with my own, his confessions were somehow like confessions for us both.

As I wait for Roland's all-clear, I gently jostle Victor behind a pillar. The pillar provides scarce cover for his immense body—rolls of flesh creasing his neck and dipping into his suit around his armpits and waist as if a giant lethargic snake had somehow coiled around him—but if somebody other than Roland comes through that door, I want to at least have a clear line of sight. Roland reappears a moment later with a wave, and I lead Victor back to my black sedan.

Clouds veil all but a few twinkling stars, and the moon has vanished again. I can smell the coastal brine in the spiraling gusts of wind.

"To the chocolate shop," Victor grunts as he wedges himself into the backseat, the dome light in the sedan momentarily causing his scalp to gleam through his thinning gray hair.

Several years ago, when Victor had told me that his wife Cora wanted to open her own sweet shop, I thought he was joking. "You're going to sell candy?" I asked.

Victor shrugged. "Cora intends to operate a small-batch chocolate boutique to help fund our retirement."

"Your retirement?"

He scratched his ear. "Evidently."

Cora picked a former real estate office with dingy, stained carpet and fake oak paneling. I was there when she badgered

Slide Crezinelli into gutting it. Back when we ran a bigger crew, Crezinelli was more accustomed to collecting bets than arguing with an old woman about redecorating. His voice, thickened by cigarettes and whiskey, made Cora's sound especially light and airy in comparison.

"I want it all out," Cora said, gesturing at the overall dreariness of the interior. Although I was still new to this world, prim Cora, her hair perfectly in place with a string of pearls around her neck, did strike me as deserving of a better backdrop. "This building is older than me. It needs old-fashioned décor, not avocado carpet and fake wood paneling. I want to restore this old lady to her former glory."

"Where's Victor?" Crezinelli asked me. "He just told me to move out the couches and desks. He didn't say nothing about gutting it. Jeez, that's a lot of work. I ain't a carpenter."

I just shrugged. "Cora's the boss here."

Cora smiled at him. "I think I'm going to name my first truffle Crezinelli's Favor." She closed her eyes and gently waved a hand in the air. "Perhaps with just a hint of cinnamon and mint. It should have a fresh minty feel but a little spice too." She opened her eyes and beamed at him. "Hmmm… doesn't that sound good?"

Crezinelli just shook his head and began ripping down the paneling, gesturing to his crew to help him. To Cora's delight, they found brick walls behind the fake wood, and beautifully stamped tin tiles above the styrofoam drop ceiling. They tore away the shabby carpet to reveal ancient oak flooring.

I visited during construction once and sat near the window in a beam of light that swirled with particles of dust. Cora sat down next to me and gave me a hug. "You should come by more often. Don't let Victor keep you too busy."

I hugged her back. "Maybe we'll see each other more when the shop opens. I have a sweet tooth, so I'll probably be your best customer."

Cora leaned back and smiled at me. "I think you just named the place, Reno. I'll call it Sweet Tooth in your honor if you don't mind."

I did start coming back over the next several weeks and helped Cora sand and wax the floors until they glowed as richly as the chocolate smelled. Granite lined the baker's kitchen in back. Cora dabbled with different recipes, but soon settled on chocolate truffles as her specialty.

Much to Roland's amusement, Cora convinced me to help decorate the truffles on Sunday mornings. After several years, I had become almost as adept in the kitchen as Cora. It's peaceful, and I enjoy gossiping with her. She's a mother to my heart.

These memories race through my mind as we drive to the Sweet Tooth. The traffic is light, and the wet streets reflect the neon lights above as rain sluices down from the night sky. When I think about Cora, I feel relaxed—or at least as relaxed as I can get.

Roland parks right outside the door. The rich smell of chocolate, mint, cinnamon, vanilla, and ginger fills my senses when we enter.

Cora comes from around the counter and embraces her husband. "I was worried something happened," she says. "It's so rainy out tonight."

Victor kisses her on the forehead. "We're fine. Sorry if I worried you."

She looks up at him. "He's here," she whispers.

My good mood instantly sours. Almost certainly she

means Carter Hansen. Cora has to be the only person who hates Carter more than Roland and me.

On the way to the kitchen, I give Cora a brief hug. "I'll stay up front," she says. Cora avoids Carter whenever she can. I wish I had the same freedom.

Carter sits hunched on a chair near the proofing room. Bloodshot eyes bulge from his face as if distended by some internal deep-sea pressure. He looks worse than usual, his sweaty skin the waxy yellow of a corpse's. Puffy lips frame his mouth. "Where you been?" he asks. "I don't like to wait."

Victor sits down across from Carter as I stand near the back door. I flick my head at Roland to stay near the front of the room.

Carter reaches into his coat and dumps photos, some folded papers, and his gold FBI badge onto the table, along with his silver inhaler. "I've got a job for you," he rasps. "Next couple days." He shoves the photos across the table. "I circled the alarm box and the hidden surveillance camera. The maintenance code for the box is written on the back."

Victor picks up the photo. "As we've discussed previously, I lack the requisite staff for this type of operation. Even with codes, we—"

Carter cuts off Victor with a wave of his hand. "Requisite staff? You fucking kill me." He coughs. "You know, I think your heart just isn't in it any more, Victor. Zhukov's eating your lunch all over town. I heard that one of his soldiers almost nailed your girl today. You got to stay strong or you're done." He sucks on his inhaler with a harsh rasp. "Look, I got a crew that can handle all the hardware." He nods at me. "I just need Reno for insurance in case something goes wrong."

"I'm not your insurance," I snap.

"You are whatever I say you are!" Carter barks. He stops abruptly and forces a smile onto his bloated face. "Look, Reno," he says tightly, "I just need a friendly face on this job."

I glare at him. "I'm not your friendly face either."

Carter spins his badge on the table. "I wish we could be friends." He shakes his head and glances at Victor. "Wouldn't it be terrible if we weren't friends?"

"We're all friends here," Victor assures him.

Carter pushes his thick lips into a pout. "Who knows what could happen if we weren't friends?" He places his hands flat on the table and examines his fingers. "I worry you could end up in trouble. Bad things happen to people all the time. You need friends to help you out."

"You assembled your own crew," Victor reasons. "I applaud your initiative. We'd probably just get in the way."

There's another long raspy hiss from the inhaler as Carter takes another hit. "You're in the way now because you won't sack up and run your own fucking crew. What the fuck is wrong with you?"

"What else do you want?" Victor asks in tired voice.

"I want us to be friends." Carter looks at me. "You need to send that cunt to charm school."

Victor sighs again. "Reno, please reassure Carter of our mutual friendship."

I grit my teeth and think of the switchblade tucked in my boot. Imagine the blade sliding into his chest and his gasp of surprise. His eyes would widen and then he would slump against me as I jammed the knife in deeper. "Sure, we're best friends."

"I'm still not getting that warm and fuzzy feeling I think I deserve." Carter stands up and drops his badge into his coat pocket. He walks over to me, so close that I can smell his rancid breath. Red veins lace his eyeballs like a fishing net.

"I bet we could be good friends if you quit fucking with me, Reno." He reaches out a hand and brushes my hair from my neck. "You know it's true. We could be real good friends."

I hold my breath and think about my switchblade.

"You know you have our full support, Carter," Victor says evenly.

Carter snorts. "Yeah, well, you have a different definition of full. And support." I glare at him until he retreats toward the back door.

"I'll set up the meeting," Carter adds. "Don't be late." He steps into the rain and slams the door.

April 14, 1973, 6:22 P.M.

"My name is Reuben."

I see a strange man arrive in the late afternoon, the sun already dipping to the horizon. He carries some strange object tethered to a lanyard around his neck. As he approaches, Papa wraps me in a hug, completely enwrapping me in his arms. He smells of fish and wood and rope, the hours spent on his boat now a permanent part of him. "Reynosa, go in the garden until he leaves," he says.

"Yes, Papa." I skip down the dock toward our garden just as the strange man steps onto the beach. He raises his hand to shade his eyes and stares at me. I crouch behind one of our banana trees and watch him back. After a moment he resumes his walk down the beach toward Papa, the object swinging from his neck.

A hummingbird flits near me, his ruby red eye close to mine. "Fly away," I whisper but he simply hovers, his blurred wings buzzing in my ear. I ignore him and focus on Papa, who hangs his head. The man has gripped Papa's shoulder and is speaking intently. Their faces are close together and my father looks sad.

But Papa almost always looks sad. Maybe he will be

happier when Mama comes back. He'll shave more often and not be so tired any more so we can play like we did before Mama left.

With his hand still grasping Papa's shoulder, the man points toward the ocean with his other hand. After a moment, Papa shrugs and nods. He still doesn't look happy.

The man hugs Papa and walks away. After a moment Papa wobbles and sits down abruptly on the dock like he's drunk again. I want to run to him, but I stay in the garden like he told me.

The man stops halfway up the beach and turns toward me. There's a smile on his tan face as he approaches my hiding place. The hummingbird darts away as the man squats on his heels.

"My name is Reuben," he says, squinting into the shadows. "Can I talk to you for a minute?"

I hesitate. I'm not supposed to strangers. I peek at Reuben from behind the fronds and see that his boots are new and his shirt is clean and not torn. He doesn't look dangerous. I step out into the open.

Reuben looks at me in the way that many men have started to look at me, and I'm suddenly shy that I'm barefoot, with just a pair of shorts and one of Papa's old shirts. I hug myself and look away.

"What's your name?"

"Reynosa."

"How old are you?"

"Almost thirteen."

Reuben's eyes track over me again. "You're very beautiful, Reynosa. Do you know that?"

It's the first time anyone but Mama has told me that I'm beautiful. I stare back at him, unsure what to say.

He unstraps the device from the lanyard and holds it up. "Do you know what this is?"

I shake my head.

"It's from the United States. It's a camera." He points it at me and presses a button. It whirs and a moment later a square tab of paper rolls from it. With a smile Reuben shakes it vigorously and holds it up for me to see. "It's called a Polaroid." I'm amazed at the sight of myself. It's a camera, but one that can instantly make a picture somehow. He slides the picture into his front pocket.

"Would you like to come back to Cartagena with me?" he asks.

I shake my head. "Papa says we have to wait for Mama to come back."

"Where did she go?"

"We don't know."

Reuben stares at me for a moment. "We can find her together," he says. "Maybe she's in Cartagena."

"Do you know Mama? Could you find her?"

Reuben puts his thumbs through his belt. "I think probably yes, we could find her if we looked hard enough."

I see that Papa is looking in my direction. He unsteadily rises and begins to walk down the dock. He no longer looks sad—I recognize the anger in his face. "You should go now," I say to Reuben. "Papa doesn't like me talking to strangers."

"We're not strangers any more, we're friends."

Papa glowers at Reuben. "I thought you were going."

Reuben nods. "One more picture." He presses a button

and another glossy square of paper emerges. He hands it to me and I shake it like he had done before, looking at it every few seconds, waiting for the image to appear.

Reuben flashes a smile at me and leaves the same way he came.

Papa and I watch him walk away. Then Papa grabs my arm, hard. Fear and anger are mixed together in his face in a way I've never seen before. "You stay away from men like that! I told you to stay in the garden, *mija*."

"Sorry, Papa." I look down at my dirty feet.

Papa takes my hand more gently and we walk through the garden into our tin and wooden house. He motions for me to sit at our small kitchen table, a salvaged wooden spool that we found on the beach after a storm.

"What did he say to you?"

"He asked me my name, that's all."

"*Todo?* What else did he ask?"

I trace my finger along a weathered crack in the spool's top. "He wanted to help me look for Mama."

Papa doesn't say anything. I look up and see tears in his eyes.

"What's wrong, Papa?"

Papa hugs me against him and I wonder why he is crying. Is it because I talked to Reuben? Or maybe it was mentioning Mama?

Papa leans back and wipes the tears from his eyes. "That man is a *narco*, Reynosa. I have to do something for him tonight. We'll talk about Mama when I return."

"Let me come with you."

"No, *mija*, it's better if you stay here. I'm leaving very late."

He looks down at me with a sad smile. "I'll be here when you wake up."

I nod, considering his words. Papa had never worked for the *narcos*. He would rather fish and maintain a modest garden than take their money. But something has changed his mind.

At dinner that night we're quiet. Papa doesn't look sad any more, at least. He appears to be thinking hard. I slide the photograph that Reuben gave to me. "Look at our picture, Papa."

We both stare at ourselves staring back from the photograph for a little while.

"How do they do that?" he asks, one blunt finger tracing my face on the photograph.

That night, Papa sits on the side of my bed and rubs my head with his calloused hand, his knotted fingers pulling at my hair. "I'm going now, *mija*. I want you to always remember that I love you and that both Mama and I are so proud and happy to have you as our daughter."

"I love you too, Papa."

He smiles, a genuine smile this time, and closes my door.

July 1, 1986, 11:47 P.M.

"You don't know shit about dogs."

Roland and I arrive at Last Call close to midnight. The place is packed, which is normal even for a weeknight. Coldest beer and best dance music in town. Both of which I like. The building used to serve as an old warehouse. It's right next to the tracks, and trains still flash by, flickering the light from the windows overlooking the river.

An old scale hangs from the wall, measuring the weight of the dancers on a wood platform next to a battered ancient piano. Jack is pouring drinks at the bar, which holds down the opposite end of the building. Roland sees me looking at Jack and flashes me his usual smirk, but I don't care.

"You going to actually talk to Jack tonight?" asks Roland.

"I talk to him all the time," I say in a tone of bored deflection. But I know from experience Roland will not be deflected or even slowed down.

"No, I mean *talk* to him. Flirt with him, let him know you like him. Or kiss him. That would definitely work. It cuts through all the crap."

I fight off the urge to get up and dance. I don't want to talk to Roland about kissing Jack, who I would very much like to kiss. I can imagine it, I can think about it, but somehow I can't actually do it.

"Please don't fuck with me right now. I'm trying to be alluring."

Roland snorts.

I suck at alluring, however, and end up sulking instead as Jack pours drinks at the bar. Screw it. I jump onto the dance floor and knock the edges off for a few songs, let the exertion relax me, smooth out all the wrinkles from the day.

I dance more like a dervish than a ballerina. Especially if I have just dealt with an assclown like Carter, I need to be pretty much near exhaustion to sleep. Either that or go to bed wired and thrash in the darkness while my mind whirls through the anxieties of yesterday, today, and tomorrow. Better to whirl my body first.

I drift back to Roland's booth before my perspiration completely soaks through my blouse.

I want to try a fetching pose, but I can't imagine how you'd do that sitting down. I finally settle for a sweaty pout, which isn't much, but it's all I've got. I still can't catch Jack's eye.

"He's not coming over," I say to Roland.

"Hey, Jack!" Roland yells. "Come over here!"

"You asshole," I hiss.

Jack waves and actually walks over. He gives me a quick hug and I breathe the soft yeasty smell of beer accentuated by the sharp tang of limes. "You look happy when you dance," he says to me.

"You have the best music!" I reply. I start to smile but flatten it out when I worry that my teeth are a little too crooked.

"Thanks."

And then we just look at each other. His loose brown hair spills down his forehead into a strong, square face with a day's worth of stubble. Like a Viking in flannel. I realize too late that I'm staring and that he's waiting for us to tell him why we called him over.

"Jack, you own a dog?" Roland asks out of nowhere. "I think a dog says a lot about his owner. Big slobbery bulldogs means you're a good kisser. Dobermans mean you don't like kids."

"You don't know what the fuck you're talking about," I say.

"I know dogs, trust me on this." He looks at Jack. "I've got me a husky. Smartest dog in the world. Good-looking, too." He takes a swig from his beer bottle. "Probably not a coincidence."

I squint at him. "Since when do you have a dog?"

Roland just looks up at the ceiling, trying to look thoughtful, which is practically impossible for him. "Hmmm, now what sort of dog do you own, Reno? I bet you have—"

"You know I don't have a dog."

"Don't interrupt me. It's rude. I'm just trying to figure out if you did have a dog, what sort it would be... Maybe a greyhound. Sleek and fast."

I smile. Maybe Roland is going to actually help this time.

"But no, not a great fit." He snaps his fingers. "I've got it! You'd end up with one of those fancy show poodles, all shaved and shampooed. You know, the fussy kind that bark too much."

"I don't see Reno owning a poodle," Jack says slowly. "She's more likely to own a wolf."

"That's not a dog," Roland says.

"Don't interrupt," I say. "It's rude." Without another word, I grab Jack's hand and pull him to the dance floor. The beat pulses through me as I whirl and thrash in front of him. He moves with a powerful grace, and I can see through my half-closed eyes that he's smiling. The crowd pushes us together, and his hand rests on my hip for a moment.

Though I'm prone to dervish, I keep it under control for Jack's sake. I haven't danced with someone in a long time. It feels a little strange to synchronize my motion with his, but I like it.

Jack's hand is on my hip again and I turn into it and kiss him on the cheek. Well, I aim for his cheek but end up with my lips pressed against his ear. He leans forward and we kiss for real this time, both his hands on my hips now.

Maybe I'm alluring after all.

July 2, 1986, 7:51 P.M.

"The Russians are business, but you are in my heart."

I recline in the driver's seat, drowsy from the heat, and enjoy the evening breeze swirling through the window. One of Cora's chocolate truffles melts sweetly on my tongue.

"What's the holdup?" Roland complains. "If punctuality is so important to Victor, you would think he'd set a better example."

"Hmmmm…" I murmur in his general direction.

Roland scowls. "You don't care. You just dance all night and show up to work half-dead."

Roland blares the horn and I jerk upright. "Whathahell?" I yell through a mouth slushy with chocolate.

Roland pulls his hand off the horn. "I told Angie I wouldn't be home too late. I can't be waiting for the old man the entire night."

I wipe chocolate spit from the corner of my mouth with the back of my hand. "That's your job, dammit. Relax."

"You should have finished that damn truffle an hour ago. You just holding it in your mouth?"

I just shrug. "So?" As a kid in Colombia, I had learned to

savor anything sweet. Any candy that I managed to steal I let melt in my mouth.

"*So?* You don't think that's a little weird? Your teeth must be rotting in your fool head. Dance all night and suck on a truffle all day?" He shakes his head. "It ain't normal."

"Only way I can sleep, you idiot."

Roland snorts. "You calling me an idiot with a mouthful of day-old chocolate? Why can't you sleep?"

"Too wired after work."

"You get any last night?"

"What do you think?"

"That means no. You and Jack got to quit messing around and start fooling around. Man is too polite. I'm telling him that the next time I see him."

The door to Victor's villa opens. I turn the ignition and the engine coughs to life. Victor waddles toward me, his face darkened by an unsettling frown.

"Honk the horn again and I'll cut off your hands, Roland," Victor says as he climbs into the back seat.

"It was Reno," Roland says. "I told her to be patient, but you know how she gets."

I move the sedan through the light traffic toward Gartello's estate just outside the city border. The trip always relaxes me. I enjoy maneuvering the sedan through the softly banked curves and hills covered with white ash trees.

When we reach Gartello's mansion, I roll through the open iron gate, a patina of rust on the bars and hinges like golden moss. Several men eye the sedan as we approach the entrance to the house. I automatically note the best way to park the sedan for a quick exit, more out of habit than concern. I am among friends. Lazy friends, however, judging by how they lounge in a single group. I can't help noticing that they lack firing alleys and the cover is too scarce.

I don't recognize the guards, but Antonio Salvatore appears from the weathered wooden portico and waves at me. Gartello's old triggerman, if the old stories are true. But now more of a counselor.

"You always put a smile on the old man's face," Salvatore says to me as we climb out of the car. "He's been looking forward to this all week. All I hear is about how pretty and smart you are. His *bella*..." He hugs me.

"Did he ask about me?" Roland deadpans.

Salvatore gives Roland a small smile. "No." He glances at the guards and pauses. "Pardon me for a moment."

He walks over to the men and has a brief conversation, which results in them spreading out, two moving back into the trees. He might be old, but he doesn't miss much. Still bothers me that his men would need that sort of instruction, but everybody's always telling me that I'm paranoid.

Salvatore ushers us through the grand wooden porch and the double doors into the house, his arm around Victor.

Victor has been coming here for more than twenty years, much longer than I've been with him. Decades of cigar smoke and good Italian meals of olive oil, garlic, and oregano have permeated the entire mansion. The scent floods me with happy memories of previous visits. A faded picture of a younger Gartello and Victor hangs from the wall among other images of men and women who have filled the old man's life.

As usual, Gartello wears an old pair of trousers and a simple white shirt buttoned to the collar. His lined face creases into a smile and he murmurs, "*Bella, bella,*" as he hugs me. Hugs for Victor and even Roland, and then he waves for us to sit down.

A plate of sausage and a bowl of linguini steam on the table along with a flagon of red wine. An actual flagon, a sort of mix between bottle and decanter. Old school. A loaf of bread arrives, and we fill our plates.

"Salvatore tells me you have trouble," Gartello says.

Victor sips his wine and glances at Salvatore. "Oh?"

Salvatore silently chews his food as Gartello steadily gazes at Victor.

Victor puts down his glass. "Zhukov isn't abiding by our agreement, by the rules you put in place. One of his men nearly killed Reno yesterday."

Gartello wipes his mouth with a crisp white linen napkin. He rubs an old scar on his hand that I know occasionally bothers him when the weather changes. "You think the Russian is your trouble?"

"You have not exerted sufficient control over him," Victor says. "He doesn't decide who lives and dies."

Gartello takes a bite of linguini and chews slowly. Finally, the old man points his fork at Victor. "The Russian is not your trouble. You're being a fool—that's your problem."

Victor's eyes harden. I recognize the look and hope he remains civil and doesn't get us all killed. I try to catch Roland's attention, but he seems unconcerned and is devouring everything on the table.

"He constantly attacks me," Victor says. "He doesn't respect you, and it hurts the organization."

"Both of you kill and steal from each other without consulting me," Gartello says peevishly. "Neither of you listen anymore."

Victor's face tightens even more. "I listen to you. I'm here now asking for your advice. I go about my business as you direct, as we both agreed."

Gartello suddenly looks weary. "How long have we known each other, Victor?"

"From the beginning," Victor replies. "I was there when you met Marta, God rest her soul."

Gartello nods slowly. He does everything slowly now. He points his fork at Victor again. "And after all our time, you think you are hidden from me?" His voice shakes a little from anger. "You think it is right to hide from me?"

I don't know what Gartello is talking about but I can sense the menace. I steal a glimpse at Salvatore, looking for signs of trouble. He looks calm and relaxed. And Roland continues to wolf down his food.

Victor swallows. "Alberto, you're my dear friend."

Gartello scowls. "I heard about it for years, but always just the small rumors. And always I think that if you needed help that you would ask me. You would confide in me. You would trust me." He puts his hands on the table. "But all the time it gets worse," he says, nearly shouting. "As each day goes by, I say to myself that you will fix this or you will share it with me like old friends are supposed to do."

"Zhukov won't listen to me, only to you," Victor begins. "I can't—"

"Your trouble is not Zhukov!" Gartello snaps. "And you know it! He is just a symptom." He takes a deep breath. "The cop is your problem," he spits.

Victor's face turns ashen. Gartello looks murderous. Roland's eyes finally dart around the room. Salvatore shoots me a small frown and shakes his head a fraction. I take a small breath and hope.

Victor swallows again. "I didn't want to involve you. He could hurt you."

Gartello leans back in his chair. "So it is true."

"Yes."

"You should have told me," Gartello says quietly.

Victor shakes his head miserably. "I'm a drowning man, Alberto. I would have just dragged you down with me." He looks around the table. "We should talk alone."

"No!" Gartello slaps the table. "No more secrets. Tell me how this happened."

Victor looks over at me with a strange expression. He opens his mouth, then pauses. I pray he won't be stubborn, not now. Finally he lets out a long exhale. "He has me on tape on an old job. I got careless. Carter gave me a choice—jail or a partnership. I've just tried to survive his partnership long enough for the statute of limitations to run out."

"Any man can be broken," Gartello scolds. "We could have found a way."

"He said his death would automatically send the tape to the cops."

"We could compromise him."

"Alberto, I appreciate your offer of help and guidance, but it's nearly over. Just twenty-one more days and the tape is worthless to him."

"And then?"

"I'm done with it. Zhukov can have my entire territory, if that's what you want," Victor says. "Just leave me my neighborhood. Let me live in peace."

"And the cop? You think he will just go away?"

"Yes," Victor says in a cold voice, his calculating, dispassionate voice from years ago, before lethargy had kneaded him into a shapeless lump of dough. "Very far away."

Gartello squints at Victor. "And you just want to give all you have to the Russians? That makes no sense to me. You've told this to Zhukov?"

Victor sneers. "I'm not telling him anything. He's your dog—you command him. Give it to somebody else, if you want. I'm done with this path."

"I have sensed that within you, Victor. It would have been better if we had talked about that too. Maybe that fault sits with me." It seems that Gartello is speaking almost with relief.

"I ask for your forgiveness if I've seemed disloyal," Victor says.

"You're like a son to me, Victor," Gartello replies gently. "Never forget that. The Russians are business, but you are in my heart. I will speak to Zhukov."

"Thank you, Alberto," Victor says.

"You are certain? There is no road back."

"I want a different road."

Gartello nods. He tucks a small roll into his napkin and stands up. "Reno, I need to talk with you before you go."

I suddenly realize that I've been holding my breath and let the air flow from my lungs.

Gartello opens the door to his garden and walks out. I glance at Victor, who simply nods.

I follow Gartello into his garden, the cool night air causing me to shiver suddenly. The scent of lilacs and roses surround me. He sits on a stone bench near a small pond, his treasured koi lazily swimming at his feet. The light from a nearby lantern reflects against the tiny ripples in the water made by the burbling fish.

I sit next to him on the stone bench, which still holds some heat from the afternoon's sun. It feels good against the cool night breeze wicking the warmth from my body. "Victor meant no disrespect," I venture. "He wanted to protect you."

Gartello nods absently. "I have already talked to the Russian about these changes." He sits in silence for several moments throwing a torn scrap of bread roll into the water. "But it is not enough. Zhukov wants to hear it directly from Victor."

"If I had my way, I would kill them all," I say. "Carter, Zhukov. All of them."

"Maybe you want it all for yourself?" Gartello looks at me curiously.

I shake my head.

"Then you should put aside all thoughts of killing." He sits still for several moments. Is he done? I get up to leave, but he gently puts his hand on my knee. "Sit with me a little while longer, *bella*…" He snaps a sprig of mint growing by the bench and crushes it in his fingers. A sweet menthol scent fills the air. "Victor's pride will not allow him to bow to the Russian. He was always like that, even as a boy. Loyal and smart with a big heart but always too filled with pride and anger. Maybe if his mother had lived…" He shakes his head sadly. "Zhukov needs confirmation of this change from Victor. He fears traps and betrayals. You must go on Victor's behalf. Talk to the Russian and promise him peace. He will believe it if it comes from you."

"They just tried to kill me."

"You will have safe passage for this meeting. And you know this is the best way."

Was it the best way? I still think wiping the slate clean is the best way. A brief flash of light from the curtains catches my eye, and I see Salvatore briefly peer out from the dining room window. A moment later, two men cradling small submachine guns saunter over to the edge of the garden. I still think they stand too close together and pay too much attention to Gartello. Stupid. Threats usually lie outside the perimeter, rarely inside.

Even with Gartello's protection, going to Zhukov isn't safe. But in the long run, it was safer than waiting for him and Victor to work it out on their own. I vouch for Victor, Gartello keeps the peace, and I probably live a bit longer. Did I really have an alternative? I grab Gartello's hand. "If you think it's for the best, I'll do it."

He squeezes my fingers. "I will speak to Zhukov and arrange a meeting for you." Then he pats my knee again. "Let's keep this between us, *bella*. Victor won't understand, and I think maybe his pride will get in the way."

As I drive back to the compound, Victor maintains a stony silence. Even Roland stares moodily out the window.

April 15, 1973, 5:47 A.M.

"Never piss off Reuben."

The sky is still dark when I wake. I slide out from under my blankets and walk barefoot across the rough planks of our floor. Approaching Papa's room, I already know from the lack of snoring that he hasn't yet returned. I crack his door open an inch and peek in anyway. His bed is empty.

I chew my knuckle and look out our kitchen window. Stars speckle the sky, and the ocean is black. I pull on my shorts and sandals. Where is Papa? He said he would be back before I woke up.

The sky is beginning to brighten by the time I reach the end of our dock. No sign of Papa or his boat. I don't know what to do. Should I just wait? I gaze at the horizon, desperate to see a mast.

Nothing.

I should have gone with him.

The sand pulls at my sandals as I trot along the beach, skirting the water that crashes ashore. Gulls regard me with benign curiosity. Sometimes Papa would beach his boat up the coast a little ways if he had engine trouble or the weather got too rough. But as I round each rocky point, I find yet another expanse of empty beach.

I trudge back to the house, constantly looking back to the horizon. I keep repeating to myself that Papa will come back and I must not cry. Papa doesn't like it when I cry.

Breathless and worried, I arrive at the entrance to the garden just as the sun's rays break through the trees to shine on our tiny house. To my delight, I see the door open. Papa must have returned!

"Papa!" I yell and run up the dirt path to our weathered door, which sags a little on its hinges like it does when left open.

A man in sunglasses steps out. His lenses are like mirrors and I am momentarily startled. I don't recognize him and slide to a stop.

"Are you Reynosa?" he asks.

I can hear other people walking around the house.

"Where's my papa?"

"Come here, girl," the man says and walks toward me.

I turn and run.

"Reynosa!"

I can hear his heavy breathing as he chases me. A hand brushes against my back, fingers grasping. I swerve away and head for the garden, our banana trees flashing by.

I dive through a gap in the boards of our back fence. A hand grabs my ankle before I can stand back up.

"Got you!"

I kick with all my strength, jerk my foot free, and I'm through. Breathing heavily, I see another man running toward me from the jungle, his expression focused and angry.

Broad leaves and branches brush against me as I plunge into the jungle. I hear men thrashing around behind me.

I squat in the shadows against the broad trunk of an awarra tree and wonder where to hide. I hear the men everywhere. I quietly creep back toward the garden, toward the one place they might not look.

Papa's poison hut sits a few hundred meters from our house, just far enough so Papa felt it wasn't a danger to our goats and chickens. The door is always locked with a rusty padlock, and Papa forbade me to ever enter it. I would stand outside as he gathered the poisons to kill the rats that like to eat the fish when we dry them in the sun. But I know of a small hole below one wall. I crawled through that hole when I wanted to be alone, when missing Mama became too much and I had to cry.

I can hear the men rustling through the jungle, trying to herd me back to the house or beach. I squeeze under the wall of the poison hut, crawling on elbows and knees until I am lying on the floor, surrounded by darkness.

I can smell the metallic tang of the poisons and cover my nose with my hand, breathing lightly. Yellow bags with ESTRICNINA and PELIGROSA are stamped above pictures of dead rats. Tiny white granules lie on the wood floor. If Papa knew I came in here, he would beat me. But I don't usually stay for long, and nothing has ever happened to me.

I listen to the men shout my name and curse. I think they will go away, then I can go find Papa. I hear them shouting to each other, sometimes only feet away as they pass the hut.

After an hour, they fall silent. Maybe Papa came home and chased them away? I move slightly, trying to avoid the white crystal poison and press my ear against the wall.

Nothing.

I relax slightly.

I pick up what seems a slight whisper, and I tense just as the door is kicked in. Several men enter the hut. I dive for the hole, but they grab me.

I bite one on his arm.

"*Jueputa!*" he yells. Another man punches me in the head and tiny sparks fill my vision.

"Don't hurt her—it will piss off Reuben, and you don't want that. Never piss off Reuben."

July 4, 1986, 9:04 P.M.

"You'll hear the slowest, biggest heart on the planet."

Perspiration drips off my nose and chin as I compress toward the floor and then extend back up again, flexing my arms as smoothly as I can manage. Tiny drops of my sweat speckle the oak floor. After a minute of that, I roll onto my back for a series of stomach crunches, followed by a full stretch to preserve my flexibility and speed. I breathe out the count in each set, listening to my own breath get more and more ragged as the session continues. My shoulder burns, and my back is still sore, but I ignore the pain. Suffer and live. Get soft and die.

I'm interrupted by a harsh buzz from the door. I pad across the room and peer at the security monitor. Roland leans back and waves at the camera with a smile.

"You're early," I declare into the tiny speaker.

He shrugs back. "Maybe you're late."

Annoyed, I buzz him in and leave my door open a crack. I'm alternating one-legged squats when Roland comes in. He squints at me, then walks around my loft, strolling with his hands clasped behind his back like he's a tourist at a museum.

"You're going to scare the shit out of Jack if he ever comes over here. Get a couch or something, for God's sake. Hang up a picture. Get a plant."

I scowl at him but I have to admit my sparse furnishings aren't exactly welcoming. A small table with two chairs are the only furniture. Stretching mats, barbells, and other weights are strewn around the floor.

My bedroom is equally bare of decoration, except for a photo of an old fishing boat that looks somewhat like my father's. I loved fishing with him. Those are my only good memories—almost like dreams now, hazy and softer in detail with each passing year. Buddhists think life is a dream, nothing real. Maybe they're right.

I dive into another series of sets as Roland sits with his arms folded and his face creased with a frown. "When's the last time you got laid?" he finally asks.

"When's the last time you got kicked in the head? What's with you lately? All you do is bitch about my sex life. Just shut up."

He just shakes his head and wanders over to my kitchen. He opens my refrigerator and pokes around. "You've got more organic food in here than a hippie salad bar." He grabs a bottle and squints at the label. "Who drinks unsweetened mango juice? Seriously." He unscrews the cap and takes a sip. "Actually, pretty good."

I grab the bar bolted into the bedroom doorframe and start a series of pull-ups. "You know, I had that same dream again last night," he calls over to me.

I drop to the floor, trying to catch my breath and ignore the burning in my arms. "Which one? And don't tell me I was in it." I press my legs into a pike and hold it.

"No, not that dream," Roland says with a grin. "Which

is too bad, since that's my favorite one. I was on some sort of stage, like in a play. But the lights are blinding and I can't see anything. Not the audience, nothing. And I'm stark naked. Just staring out into the audience, but I can't see a damn thing." He stretches his arms over his head and yawns. "Weird, huh?"

"Standard anxiety dream." I lower my legs and then raise them again.

Roland nods dubiously. "Yeah, that's what Angie said. But I'm not anxious in the dream. I'm peaceful. I'm just staring into the blackness where the crowd should be and listening to the most beautiful music." He drains the mango juice and sets the empty bottle on the table. "Don't laugh, but I swear I can hear angels singing. And it's just the most fucking gorgeous sound I've ever heard in my life. It's the softest most beautiful singing ever." He hums a little and then stops. "I can't imitate it, but it's just absolutely beautiful."

"What are they singing?"

"No words, just sounds."

"Singing needs words."

"Maybe there are words but I don't speak the language."

"I'm going to shower and then we'll go."

He nods absently, still gazing out the window.

I strip in my bathroom and mentally rehearse my upcoming meeting with Zhukov as I take a quick rinse. He should be receptive, especially if Gartello has already talked to him about it. But I trust the Russians as much as a pack of rabid dogs. They could try something stupid.

I slide into some loose jeans and a sweatshirt, tuck a switchblade into my boot, and wedge a Glock 17 into my belt. I like the precision of the Glock. It has no external safeties but is virtually impossible to accidentally discharge. You could drop it from an airplane onto concrete, and the gun wouldn't blink. My kind of style.

I step into the living room. "You ready?"

"How much time to burn before Zhukov?"

"About two hours."

Roland smiles. "We can see the fireworks."

"What fireworks?"

"The reason I'm early." He opens the door for me. "This fine country that you've adopted as home is celebrating its independence tonight from a sad little island teeming with bad teeth."

I lock my door and walk down the stairs with him. The first few stars of the evening glimmer above me. "I know *why* you celebrate. But why fireworks? Nobody has ever provided a good explanation."

"Why not? Everybody likes fireworks and ice cream. Downtown puts on a show every year."

"Then I know a good spot," I say. "Not too far from Zhukov's."

I drive slowly, content to drift in the traffic. Roland smirks when I turn down Jackson Street. "Last Call?" he asks.

I nod, trying to keep my face neutral, but I feel a muscle jump underneath my cheek.

"Going to say hi to Jack?"

"Jack who?"

Roland laughs.

"This is stupid, isn't it? What if he's already with someone?"

"I saw his face when he was watching you. He's fair game."

We sit down at a small table near the emergency exit door.

Only a handful of customers occupy the bar and most of the tables are still empty. I watch Roland chat amiably with a bartender for a moment and then return with a couple beers, the bottles already speckled with condensation. He points toward a staircase in the back.

"He said Jack's on the roof."

"Well, I'll see if he needs any help."

"You do that."

I grab both my beer and Roland's, ignoring his protests, and climb the stairs. Jack is arranging some plastic chairs into a semicircle. He glances over and smiles.

Something eases in me. I'm a little stunned by how good I suddenly feel. And shy. And awkward. The usual. So I just stand there feeling like an idiot as he walks over, boots crunching in the white rock gravel. "Good to see you."

I hand him Roland's beer. "Cheers!" I never say that, but that's what comes out of my mouth.

We stand there and sip our beers. A sliver of moon floats on a bank of clouds on the horizon. I think of my father every time I see the moon. He once told me that the moon shines with the souls of the dead. *Their spirits light up the heavens, mija.* The normal cacophony of the city had subsided, with just a few pops of firecrackers in the distance breaking the hush. At this moment, for the first time in forever, I am at peace.

"To grace and beauty," Jack says, holding his beer aloft.

I shrug and clink my bottle against his. "I'd hardly call this area beautiful."

"I was talking about you."

I sip my beer and search for something smart and flirty. Nothing comes. I contemplate jumping off the roof.

"See those blinking dots?" he says, rescuing me from the awkward silence. He points to a pair of gleaming white lights moving swiftly across the darkening sky.

I nod, still waiting for something witty to come. Willing now to settle for anything besides idiotic silence.

"Satellites," Jack says. "Probably belong to the defense department. They can take our picture with enough clarity to see my sunburn."

I squint at the fleeing pair of lights. "How do you know they're satellites?"

"Speed of transit and lack of aeronautic beacons rule out aircraft. Plus a tandem pair like that usually means surveillance of some kind." He shrugs and smiles. "But still kind of an educated guess."

"Can they really take our picture?"

"Absolutely." He puts his arm around me and raises his beer toward the sky. "Say cheese!"

Surprised by his quick hug, I instinctively pivot on my heel to spin away but catch myself just in time. I hoist my own beer, hoping he didn't catch my reaction. Relax. Chill.

Jack steps away and sits down on a chair. "So what do you do when you're not dancing or getting photographed by satellites?"

I lean on the railing that encircles the roof. "I make chocolates part-time. Mostly truffles. Handmade in a little shop downtown."

He nods. "A chocolate chef, eh? Nice."

"Not really a chef. More like an assistant to the chef. You?"

He takes another swig. "Mostly just bartend. I surf in the mornings if the break is good. You surf?"

I shake my head. "I can't swim very well."

He cocks his head. "Can't swim?"

"I can swim, just not good enough to surf."

"Just stay on the board. You should get somebody to teach you."

"Know anyone?" I tease, finally relaxing a little bit.

He smiles at me. "Yeah, I think I do."

A voice from behind us interrupts. "Jack?"

The bartender from downstairs, who looks harassed and exasperated, is poking his head over the edge of the roof.

"Yeah, Felix?"

"It's getting busy down there. Are you serious about letting people up here?"

"Only the sober ones. Hang on, I'll be right down." He turns to me. "You sticking around for the fireworks?"

I nod.

He smiles. "Good. I'll see you later."

A few minutes later, people start awkwardly clambering over the railing and onto the roof, many spilling their drinks but not caring. Laughter and conversation drifts around me. Eventually, Roland saunters up and together we watch the bright blossoms of pyrotechnics erupt over our heads. I enjoy the percussion of the shells almost as much as the sparkling shower of sparks and embers that stream toward the ground.

I'm surprised that Jack actually lets people onto the roof, but he herds them away from the edge like a sheepdog. A part of me admires his athletic grace as he flows among the crowd, but a larger part anxiously reviews my upcoming meeting with Zhukov, probing my plan for flaws.

Old man Gartello had set up the meeting, so it seems unlikely that Zhukov will attempt any treachery. Not out of honor, I know, but just for the pragmatics of survival. I'm not worth the trouble.

I look forward to Victor's retirement and a presumably safer lifestyle for us both. I doubt that he'll retire completely, but I welcome any change that reduces the time I'd have to spend with Zhukov, Carter, and a host of other assholes.

The whistles and clapping for the finale bring my attention fully back to the rooftop. I smell cordite from the drifting clouds of smoke, which glow slightly from the reflection of the city lights below. The music kicks up a notch, the beat pulsing through the roof and into the soles of my feet as the crowd disperses back down to the club.

I walk over to Jack as he cheerfully waves the last group down the ladder.

"Were you serious about learning to surf?" he says.

"I'd probably drown trying to learn."

"I wouldn't let that happen. Besides, you can't avoid water your whole life. Where's the fun in that?"

I hug myself, suddenly chilled. "True."

"Plus it's good for the heart," he adds. "Surfers have the slowest heartbeats in the world."

"Bullshit," I laugh. "Marathoners and yoga masters have way slower heartbeats."

"Listen for yourself," Jack says playfully and pushes out his chest. "You'll hear the slowest, biggest heart on the planet."

"You're bluffing."

Jack points at his heart. "Try me."

My own heart beating rapidly now, I step closer to him and press my left ear to his chest. His heartbeat, *lub-dub, lub-dub,* fills my ear and I hug his chest tighter, mesmerized by its sound and the smell of Jack's perspiration and a faint cologne of leather and tobacco. His slow heartbeat somehow reassures me.

A voice echoes from the edge of the roof. "So what's all this?"

I quickly step away.

A small-framed woman with her red hair tied into a ponytail stands at the head of the stairs leading to the roofline. "Am I interrupting something?"

"Carmen, this is Reno," Jack says. "I'm going to teach her how to surf."

A brittle smile creases Carmen's face. "Is that so?"

"She dances here sometimes," Jack adds awkwardly.

"I'm Jack's partner," Carmen says, extending her hand.

"Carmen arrived in town yesterday," Jack adds quickly.

I can feel myself blushing. Carmen has an air of possessiveness, and I suddenly feel out of place. And what the fuck does "partner" mean?

"Jack, you got a moment to talk privately?" Carmen says.

"I have to go anyway," I say before Jack can reply.

"Wait, Reno—" Jack says, but I don't stop.

July 4, 1986, 10:17 P.M.
"I devour my enemies like lions eat."

I jam the sedan into gear and fishtail out of the Last Call parking lot then lurch to a stop to avoid running over an elderly couple holding hands in the crosswalk. They scurry back to the curb, glaring at us.

I slam my hands against the steering wheel. "Shit!"

I summon a thin smile and wave for them to cross. The woman shakes her head and gives me the finger.

Roland cheerfully flips her off in return. The man immediately copies the gesture with an angry stab. And so I flip him off and all four of us scowl at each other for a moment before I punch the accelerator and leave them behind. Screw them. Screw Jack. Screw Carmen. Screw everyone.

"You okay?" Roland asks, holding tightly to the door handle as I take a sharp corner and careen onto the wrong side of the street. Approaching cars veer right and blare their horns.

"Fine," I grunt as I muscle the sedan back into our lane. "I'm fine."

"That's what I thought," Roland says. "Just confirming."

"He's an asshole," I say.

"I'm sure he is."

I should have never let my guard down. Look at me now. These sorts of distractions just make my job more dangerous. "I should've stuck to our plan."

"What plan?"

I glare at him. "The plan. The first one."

"Okay."

"I mean not visiting. Just waiting someplace else."

"I didn't know that was the plan. It was your idea to see Jack."

"I know. You were early. Shut up."

Roland shakes his head.

"Beauty and grace," I mutter to myself. "Such bullshit."

Roland shifts in his seat. "I don't know what just happened, but I was serious about what I said back in the hospital. You got to find a different worldview, or life is going to chew you up."

I take a deep breath and try to calm myself. "I'm fine."

"Angie and the baby make it better for me," Roland says. "Somebody to help take the edge off, care for, make me think about other things. You should let the universe love you."

"It's not that easy for me," I say glumly.

We drive in silence for several minutes. I slow the sedan as we enter a neighborhood dominated by Russian restaurants and businesses. "Welcome to Little Moscow," I breathe. "We'll cruise by and check it out."

We coast up to Zhukov's café, and I double-park the sedan with the driver's side facing the tables.

"Okay, I think we're on," I say to Roland. "If something stupid happens, do me a favor and shoot Zhukov first."

"If it goes bad, stay low and try to go left toward the light pole," Roland says. He pulls a snub-nosed Uzi from beneath the seat and checks the magazine. "You sure about this?"

I nod.

"If it goes shitty, I'll get you," he says. "I'll always bail you out. Don't ever forget that."

I'm filled with a sudden warmth toward him. "Roland, you're the best friend I have."

His smile goes crooked. "Then you need better friends. I'm a murderous criminal with a prison record."

"Birds of a feather," I snort and step out of the sedan.

As I approach the café, the men standing around the door straighten. I sit down at a small table near the street. A moment later, Zhukov walks out of the café with another man. The bodyguard's face snaps into my memory—the bastard who hit me with his car. He approaches me with a swagger, his squat physique rippling with muscle, and gestures for me to stand up. I get to my feet and he roughly pats me down, squeezing my breasts with two hands as I seethe. As I expected, he finds my Glock and hands it to Zhukov, but my switchblade is still nestled in my boot.

Zhukov's close-cropped hair, dyed titanium white, glows in the streetlights. He sits down across from me and places my Glock on the table between us. "You are beautiful woman." He strikes a match and cups his hand around a cigarette to light it. The flare of his match briefly shadows his eyes and brow, creating a mask of dark and light. He takes a heavy drag on the cigarette and blows out a plume of smoke.

Zhukov's bodyguard stares at Roland in the sedan with sullen displeasure. Roland gives us all a jaunty wave.

I flick my eyes up to the bodyguard. He's wearing a tight

black shirt, buttons undone to his chest, the golden links of a chain nestled in a mass of hair. "This is a private conversation," I say.

He doesn't move. I try to stare him down, unblinking. Was he the driver of the car that hit me? I didn't see the driver clearly, but I've seen this guy before. But I can't remember the circumstances or why he would harbor such an anger toward me.

Zhukov squints at me, his eyes crinkled in amusement. "No such thing as privacy any more. Please let me introduce Golnak. He's a, what you say, a valued associate. You can trust him."

"Humor me."

Zhukov regards me with a thoughtful look and then waves a hand. Golnak gives me a lingering flat stare but moves far enough away to satisfy me. I think Gartello's involvement still provides amnesty, but I scoot my chair slightly to the left anyway, giving Roland a better angle.

"Gartello tells me fairy story," Zhukov says. "Says you have truce offer, that Victor wishes peace. But I think maybe you want job instead before I kill you both."

I hesitate. "You think I'm here for a job? Working for you?"

Zhukov nods. He inhales another drag from the cigarette, its tip becoming a red ember. "You sell us Pagnolli for trade to join."

"I'm not here to sell you Victor," I scoff. "Gartello asked me to convey a message. That's it."

He shrugs and spins the pistol. The barrel twirls between us. "But maybe lie."

"I don't lie," I say.

He leans forward, a sudden interest in his face. "Maybe

then we comrades. I also tell no lies. My men will tell you that I always say things as they are. Never what I wish, only as things exist."

I see genuine pride on Zhukov's face. "You never lie?" I say. "About anything?"

Zhukov flicks his ashes downwind and nods. "Ask me questions for test."

"Did you send Golnak to kill me two days ago?"

"No."

"No? I'm pretty sure he was driving the car that hit me."

Zhukov shrugs. "You ask question wrong. He send himself. I know nothing until after." He inhales again, the cheeks puckering slightly from the pressure. "Ask more."

I glance over at Golnak, who lingers in the shadows. "Why did he try to kill me?"

Zhukov shouts something to Golnak in harsh Russian. *"Počemu vy pytaetes' ubit' ee?"*

Golnak spits out a reply, and the other men laugh. His guttural accent carries across the terrace like a coughing dog. Zhukov replies in an even harsher voice. Golnak walks over and explains in rapid Russian as the other men silently listen in. He speaks to Zhukov in a low voice, darting angry glances at me.

Zhukov drums his fingers on the barrel of my gun. "He claims you strike him while dancing. Injure arm." He hesitates, searching for the right word. "And you insult the feelings inside him."

I frown, trying to make sense of it. I look back at Golnak, who yawns wide in response, exposing his teeth to the gums. They are a train wreck of chipped enamel and blackened fillings. Suddenly the memory floods back. I was dancing in a club downtown. The dance floor was crowded, with some inadvertent pushing. Eyes half closed, I wasn't paying much attention to the bumps until an insistent hand grabbed me by the back of the neck. I spun around, breaking the grip, and saw a sweaty man wanting to dance. I pushed him back, shaking my head in a firm but polite decline. And he just smiled, revealing his ruined smile. I closed my eyes again, trying to regain the flow of the music, only to feel a hand on my neck again, harder now and more insistent.

My temper has always been quick. After fighting with a barrio child or arguing with my mother, I would sulk for hours. My father would cheer me up by quietly fashioning little dolls from twigs or bits of twine in his pocket with hands made nimble by decades of weaving fishing nets. I would tearfully explain that I didn't start the fight, that I had just lost control of my anger. He would always hug me and say in his soft voice, "Short patience brings long regrets, *niña*."

Maybe I would have learned patience if my father had lived longer. After his death, the people I met were hardly the type to give me hugs or gentle advice. And so when the strange man with the broken teeth grabbed for me again, I stepped into his arms and crushed my knee into his groin. He grunted and fell sideways onto the dance floor, propping himself with one hand. The other dancers backed away, uncertain. I took a short step and kicked his elbow out as he started to rise to his feet. He crashed back to the floor with a scream. I left the club never to return, favoring the Last Call from that night on.

"I remember him now," I say. "He was rude. So I broke his arm."

Zhukov motions Golnak away and then looks at me

thoughtfully. "Almost one years before, yes? Many months for his arm to heal. It create in him, what is it you say? A grudge in his heart. I think maybe he will not forgive."

I shrug. "I gave him a chance to reconsider and he made the wrong choice."

"Golnak knows the world in only simple ways." He flicks his cigarette into the darkness. The embers flare into tiny sparks as the cigarette tumbles across the sidewalk. "I think his head suffer injury when a child."

I try to get back on track. "Victor is offering a truce. You'll get his territory without any fighting if you can just wait a little while. Gartello agrees to this too."

"He gives what he knows I can take."

"It might not be as easy you think," I gaze at him steadily. "And you owe more respect to Gartello. Without him you would be nowhere."

Zhukov idly taps his index finger on my gun. "It is true. Which is why I sit here, even though many say I should just take what I can, and not bow to an old man."

"Sit and gain what you want for no risk, no work."

Zhukov steeples his hands in front of his nose. "In Africa the lion and hyena fight each other. Never do they stop. I think maybe Pagnolli also cannot stop. You tell me he stops, but words do not last. He has robbed me of many things and killed men who matter to me."

"You have my word and Gartello's," I say. "We will leave you alone if you leave us alone. And eventually you'll have the entire city for yourself."

"Why does Victor run away? I wonder about this offer." Zhukov picks up my Glock and cocks it, letting the barrel drift upward toward the stars. "Why not Victor say these things to me? Why only do you say them?" He looks at me suspiciously, the barrel glinting in the street light.

"He's too proud. He'll do it, but he won't say it. Not to you."

Zhukov uncocks the gun and puts it back down on the table. "And after? Will you join the lions or keep running with the hyenas?" He slides the gun across to me. "You think what you will do."

I nod and pick up my gun. As I walk back toward Roland, Zhukov calls after me.

"Reno! If you have told me lies, the business will become personal to me."

I give him the finger and slide into the sedan.

I can hear his laughter as we pull away.

July 6, 1986, 2:37 A.M.

"Toss me the stripper!"

For once my insomnia actually comes in handy. It's the middle of the night, and I'm wide awake waiting for that asshole Carter. He's late as usual, but finally I see his rusty Cadillac cruise down the avenue toward me. The streetlights give it the color of dried blood.

Carter kicks open the passenger door. I slide in, regret already burning my veins like snake venom.

"Hey Carter, how's—"

A harsh rasp interrupts me as Carter presses his bright aluminum inhaler to his mouth. His eyes bulge from the pressure as he sucks on the canister. The usual sheen of sweat covers his face, and his puffy lips make me think of a ghastly deep-sea fish in a rancid checkered sports coat. I look away to hide my disgust.

When I look back, his face is a bloated purple. Without thinking, I put my hand on his shoulder. "Hey, are you okay?"

Carter slaps my hand from his shoulder, face contorted into a grimace. He takes another hit from his inhaler. "You ready?" he gasps, flushed and doused with perspiration.

I just stare at him.

Carter looks back, perplexed. "What are you looking at?"

"I thought you were going to die from a seizure or something," I say.

"Just sit for a minute and give me a little courtesy, okay? I'm a sick man." He takes a final suck on his respirator and puts the Caddy in gear. "Open the window, would you?"

I roll down the window.

Carter mutters and swears to himself as he pilots the Cadillac downtown. Sprinklers shower some of the lawns we pass.

"Where's your crew?" I finally ask. "It's not just you and me, is it?"

Carter barks out a laugh. "They don't like my driving. They're meeting us there."

I stare out the window again, regretting the whole idea once again and hoping that Victor really has found a way to rid of us Carter.

I don't trust the situation. Too many new people. But they have the sense to not ride with Carter, which is more than I could say for myself at the moment.

"I'll be your pail of sand in case you catch fire," Carter says.

"And how exactly are you going to put us out if something goes wrong?" I ask.

Carter digs into his coat and pulls out his badge. "If I show up, just play along."

He pulls into a narrow alley near downtown. Still muttering to himself, he peers around a row of dented dumpsters. "She should be here," he says. "Crazy bitch…"

The place looks abandoned to me, and I don't like idling so close to the job. Any passing cruiser would notice. Just then a face rises up from below Carter's window and hisses "Boo!" right in his face.

Carter flinches back, almost cracking my teeth with the back of his head. "Shit!"

Whoever startled Carter is giggling. I lean over and see someone bent over with laughter.

"Very funny, Carmen," grumbles Carter. "I'm back in ten minutes. That's all the time you have. If my lights are on, let me drive by. If they're off, hop in when I stop."

I barely hear any of that. I peer intently at the figure now slouched against a dumpster. Carmen? I must have misheard him. Was that her? Confused and concerned, I open the door and step out.

Carter steps on the gas and roars away.

When she sees my face, she startles almost as badly as Carter. Her look of surprise and anger makes me take a step back. "Remember me?" I ask.

"Of course. You're the bitch Jack wants to fuck." Right then I decide we're probably never going to be friends.

And speak of the devil, Jack appears from around the corner. "Oh." Confusion scrambles his face.

"A bartender, huh," I say.

"Yeah, I'm sorry if we're taking you away from your chocolate recipes."

I guess he has a point. "I did leave some parts of my job out."

Carmen shakes her head. "Jesus. Give me a break. We've got to get going." She steps into the darkness of the alley, leaving Jack and me alone for a moment.

Jack steps closer to me. "You didn't give me a chance to explain on the roof," he says softly.

"Whatever. You don't owe me an explanation."

"Jack, what the fuck you doing?" Carmen hisses. "Come on!"

Jack holds up his hand. "Hang on." He steps toward me. "Carmen's a business partner now," said Jack. "That's all."

I raise an eyebrow. "Now?"

He shrugs. "Complicated. Can I explain later?"

"Don't bother." But I do want him to explain.

He sighs, hands me a leather satchel, and strides over to the sidewall of the jewelry store, directly below the alarm box and the phone line. After brushing the alley grit from his palms, he slips his hands into leather gloves. Carmen tosses me a pair and then we all cover our faces with black masks. Victor's rules.

Jack cups his hands into a stirrup and nods to Carmen. She lightly steps into his clasped hands and he boosts her up into the air, swiveling to press her upward so they both lean against the wall. Jack sways and grunts with the exertion as Carmen carefully places one foot onto his shoulder, and then the other. They've clearly done this before.

I peek down the alley, make sure nobody is watching us.

Carmen directs him to slide over a few feet so she can grab the roof gutter for balance. "Toss me the stripper," she hisses to me.

I don't know what she is talking about.

"Look in the satchel," Jack says. "There should be a wire stripper in there somewhere."

I root around in the satchel and retrieve the wire stripper and loft it to Carmen, who deftly snatches it in mid air. She strips back the sheathing around the cable to the phone box a few seconds later.

"Circuit board," Carmen huffs.

I find a wrapped circuit board and toss it to Carmen.

"I embedded Carter's maintenance code into EPROM," Jack says to me. "It should fool the monitoring software back at the alarm company, at least for a little while."

Carmen quickly crimps the wires into the phone lines. "Okay, give me the thermos!" she whispers to me.

I flip it up to her. "Heads up!"

Carmen nimbly catches the thermos and carefully unscrews the cap. She feels along the top of the alarm box and tips the thermos into a vent. I hear the gurgle and fizz of freezing plastic and metal strands. Smoking liquid drips from a crack in the casing and falls to the pavement. I think maybe she used liquid nitrogen but really have no idea. Jack yelps and steps away, eliciting a curse from Carmen as she fights for balance.

"Watch it!" Jack grumbles. "Don't spill that shit on me."

Carmen laughs softly. "Oh, you big baby." She gestures toward me. "Throw me the air."

I find a can of compressed air in the satchel and lob it to her. Carmen fits the nozzle into the casing vent and shoots a blast of air into the alarm case. A puff of shattered copper and plastic blows out, drifting to the ground like a cloud of falling stars.

No clanging tonight, I think. I glance at the circuit board. No lights, no nothing.

Jack catches Carmen as she drops to the ground.

"Okay, next step," Jack says. "I'll take care of the window." He gestures to the circuit board. "Keep an eye on that," he says to me. "It should light up all green in a minute. If you see anything red, tell me."

He grabs the satchel from me, walks over to the display window, and pulls out a small plunger with a two-foot-long wire dangling from it. Jack centers the plunger on the window and rapidly works the lever on its plunger. The cup sucks tightly against the glass, which is slightly fogged from his labored breathing.

He pulls out some contraption that looks like a wand and presses it against the glass at a slight angle and drags it in a wide arc until he's etched a complete circle. The gritty sound of sliced glass vibrates in my ears. Has to be a diamond-edged cutter or something. Using diamonds to steal diamonds. He taps experimentally around the etched arc. A few moments later, I hear a sharp *pop-crack*, and the silvered edge of a gap in the glass glimmers in the streetlight. Jack follows it around the arc, tapping as he goes. With a sharp *crack!* he completes the circle and pulls it from the window. The weight of the glass must have surprised him, because he loses his grip and it shatters, throwing shards of glass across the sidewalk like silver sparks.

"Shit!" He dances back into the alley.

I point at the dangling circuit board, the night breeze causing it to rock back and forth. "Thar she blows," I whisper. The lights on the board blink in the night like a constellation of small green stars. *Carter actually got it right,* I think with some amazement. Whatever code Jack plugged in must have worked.

"All green indicates matching codes, the wafer telling each system to disregard the signals as long as the maintenance code exists," Jack says. I have no idea what any of that means.

"Still doubting our friend Carter?" Carmen asks. "I told you he had this place nailed."

"I have no doubt he's an asshole," Jack says.

She cuts him a hard look. "At least I can count on him."

"Give it a rest, Carmen," Jacks says irritably, which cheers me up a little. "Let's go. Give a shout if any of those lights turn red, Reno." They turn back around the corner, broken glass crunching under their feet. I stare up at the circuit board and pray that they'll be quick.

Two minutes later, they're back in the alley, just as a pair of oncoming headlights sweep around the corner. I curse our luck, but then its lights wink off and I realize that it's Carter's Cadillac.

Another surprise. He's timed his arrival perfectly. He kicks the door open as he pulls alongside us.

"Get in the fucking car," hisses Carter.

"No way," Jack says.

Carter looks at me. "Get in."

"I'm with Jack," I say. "We'll meet you at the junkyard. I'll show them the way."

Carter curses and stomps on the gas.

"Follow me," Jack says. We troop down the alley for a half block. Parked in the shadows is a battered old Pontiac. Jack opens the door and in a moment we're smoothly easing out of the alley and onto the adjoining street.

Jack lets out a long breath and pulls off his knit mask. "We good?" he asks Carmen.

"Bordering on excellent," she says in a husky voice, sounding almost euphoric with adrenaline.

Jack drives to the outskirts of town, all the windows rolled down to create a breeze. I direct him to the junkyard where Oscar Munoz and his men strip cars, most legitimate but many not, among the other services they perform for Victor. The last of our muscle, really, since Victor's crew has dwindled to almost nothing over the last few years, much to Carter's disappointment and my alarm.

I don't know what to say to Jack, so I'm happy for the moment that the roar of the wind would drown out any conversation. I just point the way at each intersection until we reach the junkyard. It sprawls next to an old cemetery, only a heavy chain-link fence separating the rows of tombstones from the rusting carcasses of dead cars.

Jack wheels up the dirt road leading to the entrance, the dry dust floating through the open windows and covering us like a fine talcum. I climb out and stretch, smelling my sour perspiration. The wind carries the hint of carnations and lilies from the graveyard.

Carter has already arrived; his car sits empty, the hot engine still ticking. No doubt he's inside badgering Victor.

"Let's celebrate," breathes Carmen as she steps out of the car. "Champagne and chocolate and music. All the things I couldn't have for the last five years."

"No party for me," Jack says. "I'm beat."

Carmen glares at him. "You going out with her instead?"

I just shake my head and lead them toward the warehouse.

"I didn't know Reno was coming," Jack protests. "Carter just said he was bringing along some help. A babysitter."

"We don't need babysitting," Carmen says. "You, me, and Carter—that's all we need."

"I don't want to do this anymore," Jack says. "Especially not with Carter."

"What's wrong with Carter? So he's a little fucked up."

"A little?"

I listen to them argue as we wind our way through the stacks of crushed cars to a warehouse slowly disintegrating from a combination of rust and neglect. We use the junkyard as a sort of office for all sorts of things.

I open the door into the warehouse. Men in bandannas create tiny crackling thunderstorms of white lightning with their arc welders as they dissect the husks of stolen cars. Grinders shoot hornets of yellow and gold into the hot air. Whistles and grins greet me as I walk through the shop. I flip them all off with a friendly grin, which of course elicits even more catcalls.

The acrid fumes of gasoline and old motor oil sting my nostrils as I survey the warehouse floor. Axles, frames, and engines lie on the floor like bones excavated from the stained cement.

I yank open a small wooden door smeared with countless handprints of grease and dirt. Victor sits in the dimly lit room at a desk strewn with papers. Hammers, crowbars, pneumatic drills, and other construction equipment fills the rest of the space. Roland is leaning against the far wall. We nod at each other.

"What did I tell you, Victor?" Carter crows as I shut the door. "Told you I had this job nailed." Carmen takes this as a cue to spill the contents of her two bags onto the desk. Gemstones flash in the slanting shafts of light that can penetrate the dirty windows.

Victor picks up a necklace and holds it aloft. "Yes, you nailed it, Carter." He tilts his head toward Jack and Carmen. "Introduce me to your friends."

"They're my new crew. Carmen and Jack. We're going to make a hell of a team."

"Indeed." Victor struggles out of his chair and extends a hand to Jack. "Call me Victor." He nods to Carmen.

"Splendid." He eyes the mound of gems. "Probably close to fifty after fence. It'll take a week to move it."

"Small fry," Carter says. "But our next job is a huge one. I'm getting wood just thinking about it." He smiles at us, revealing narrow little teeth and heightening my impression that he's some sort of dangerous fish surfacing from a great depth. "I'm excited. And I don't excite easy."

A scowl of irritation crosses Victor's face. "Oh?"

Carter nods vigorously. "The pieces just fell into place last night. I know a guy who can get me into the customs dock where a load of Beluga caviar will be waiting for us. A whole container. Those little fish eggs are worth more than coke. Those goddamn Soviets keep poisoning the Caspian Sea and every year they get fewer eggs. The price is skyrocketing, almost a thousand bucks an ounce."

I notice that Carmen's mouth is slightly open. Her face is flushed with the same look of rapture that she had earlier. Adrenaline junkie.

Victor slowly nods, considering. "What's the job?" he finally asks. "Getting into customs is the easy part. Getting out is the hard part."

Carter laughs. "That's the beauty of it. We're robbing the robbers. Their shell company gets the insurance, and the Russians fence their own stolen eggs. I'm telling you, they're genius at that sort of shit." He takes a quick hit on his inhaler. "They just switch manifests, repaint the container to match, and presto, they just wheel through customs. The drivers don't even know what's going on. We've got about four hours between crews when we can grab the caviar ourselves. There's no way to screw this up if we're quick. I got myself a moonlighting security job in the next warehouse over, so I'll be able to handle any emergencies." He laughs again. "And what are they gonna do? Complain to the police?"

"Interesting," Victor muses.

"And it gets even better," Carter says. "We'll be screwing over Zhukov."

"No!" I blurt out without even thinking.

The entire room looks at me.

"Who asked you?" Carter spits.

"What's wrong, Reno?" Victor asks.

I can feel my face redden. "I don't think we should screw with Zhukov," I say. "And Gartello won't like it, either," I quickly add.

"It's all lined up," continues Carter, ignoring me. "I'm just waiting for the shipment. My guy will let me know."

"What guy?" asks Victor, still curiously looking at me.

"One of your old crew. Ivan Chopek."

"We can do this alone," Carmen says. "Jack can drive a rig. We don't need Reno."

"We need to talk about this," Jack says in a low voice, clearly irritated. "This is the first I've heard about it."

"I think we can make it work," Carmen says.

Jack shakes his head. "I have to think about it." He stuffs his hands in his pockets and walks out of the room.

I follow Jack with Roland gliding beside me, his big frame floating effortlessly along the cement floor. The squall of metal cutters and the shouts of the men fill the air.

Roland taps Jack on the shoulder. "Hey, it's my favorite bartender. Small world, huh?"

Jack nods. "Guess so."

Roland smiles, crinkling the webbing of old cuts and

scars that surround his eyes. "I didn't figure you hanging with Carter."

"You either," Jack says and picks up his pace.

Roland nudges me, and I take a quick couple strides and catch up.

"Hey, Jack?"

Skepticism and anger cloud his face. "What?"

As usual, I still don't know what to say. "Never mind."

He shakes his head and keeps walking.

April 16, 1973, 1:47 P.M.

"Don't bite me."

The surf pounds against the rocks as my eyes strain toward the horizon for Papa's boat. The sting of brine fills my nose and I squint into the sun, which flashes again and again. Then I abruptly wake up. The pounding of the surf is just my head throbbing, and the sun is Reuben taking pictures of me with his Polaroid.

I sit up on the cold cement floor and grab my head. Water drips from the rusty corrugated roof. Reuben's sitting on an old battered sofa, the golden fabric faded and ripped. The cushions are stained with what might be blood.

"I'm sorry my men hit you," Reuben says. He smiles but his eyes don't change.

I stand on wobbly legs and a bolt of pain shoots through my temple.

"Did you bite him?" asks Reuben.

I nod.

"Still no excuse. He won't hurt you again." He sets the camera on the floor and stands up. He hugs me and I smell sweat and gasoline and the barest remnants of something sweet. I try to push away but he just hugs tighter and I start to cry.

"Sshhhh," he murmurs and pulls me toward the couch.

I strain to break free, but my feet just scrape against the cement floor as he drags me across the room. He tosses me onto the couch and then flops down on top of me, his weight pushing the air from my lungs.

"Don't bite me," Reuben says and digs his knee into my chest as I gasp for air.

Through teary eyes I watch him unsling his belt from around his hips. Then he wraps his belt around my head and across my mouth, crushing my lips against my teeth. He roughly rolls me onto my stomach and rips off my shorts.

I scream and scream and scream.

Afterward I lie on the couch and listen to his Polaroid flash and whir.

"Grab your shorts," Reuben says. "It's time to go."

I stare at the floor. A tiny ant wanders across the cement.

He throws my shorts at me. "Let's go!"

The door slams and I am alone. I slip on my shorts and listen to the water drip from the rusty roof. A moment later the door creaks open and footsteps approach. Rough hands pull me up and drag me outside, the sun squeezing my eyes shut. I leave my feet and I'm tossed into the bed of a pickup. The truck lurches forward and I roll onto my back. A gull wheels above me, momentarily rimmed by the sun.

After a while, I smell the putrid decay of garbage and the sky is filled with gulls. Brakes screech to a stop and doors slam. The tailgate slams down. While I continue to stare at the sky, hands grab my ankles and pull me down the rusty bed of the truck and I flop into the mud and garbage.

The truck pulls away, its spinning wheels spattering me with the filthy muck. Tears flow no matter how tightly I close my eyes.

Sometime later I hear hushed voices around me. I hope whoever it is goes away and leaves me alone. I get my wish and lie in the sun for several more hours. The mud slowly dries and I feel like I'm wrapped in a shroud and waiting to die.

Tiny fingers gently scrape mud from my face. I open my eyes and see a young girl with filthy hair and skin staring at me, her face inches from mine.

"What are you doing?" she asks.

I just stare back.

After a moment she runs away. I close my eyes, but in minutes she is back.

"Here," she says.

I open my eyes again. She's brought an older boy who's looking at me suspiciously. A dirty red tank top and too-large pants hang from his skinny frame. Lank hair droops down his forehead almost to his eyes.

"The men dropped her on the ground and drove away," the girl says.

The boy quickly looks around. "What men?"

"Gone now," the girl says. "Drove away."

"What did they look like?"

"I don't know."

"What were they wearing?"

"I don't know." The little girl crosses her legs and hugs herself.

"Never mind. Go tell Miguel and bring some water—can you do that?"

She nods and runs off.

He squats next to me. "You okay?"

I close my eyes.

"Where are your pants?"

I ignore him.

"You shouldn't just lie here. Bad things can happen to you."

"Bad things already happened to me."

"I know. What's your name?"

"Reynosa."

"My name is Pablo. If I can get you home, do you think your parents will give us some money? For helping you?"

I sit up, rubbing the mud from my eyes and mouth. "I don't live here. But maybe my mother does. Is this Cartagena?"

Pablo shakes his head. "The toilet of Cartagena." He stretches from his squat and stands up. "Do you have any money?"

I shake my head.

"Can you steal?"

The pain when I stand is intense. I let the air from my lungs hiss between my teeth. "No, I don't steal," I say when the pain ebbs.

"That's okay," Pablo says. "I'll teach you. But remember that Miguel gets half."

July 7, 1986, 5:47 P.M.

"You going to show me your panties?"

I jerk awake with a gasp, adrenaline burning through me. I lunge to one side and crack my chin on the window. My hand clubs the steering wheel, momentarily setting off the horn. I look around wildly and see Roland regarding me with amusement.

"Hey, relax," he says. "You got a hair trigger on you, girl." He pulls on a cigarette, his cheeks hollowing slightly. "You nap so much that I'm starting to think you're up all night having circus sex. Or maybe you're some crazy electro-sexual."

I rub my chin and blink at him. "Electro-sexual?"

Roland laughs. "You know, loving a buzz puppet?"

I look at him blankly.

"Steely Dan?"

I shake my head, still bewildered.

"Wonder worm? Battery-operated boyfriend?"

"Your obsession with my sex life is creeping me out. Just mind your own business."

"Oh, never mind." He's holding a hotdog in one hand and a cigarette in the other. He blows a plume of blue smoke into the flat afternoon light. A passing diesel truck swirls the smoke into nothing and flaps his hair, momentarily revealing his scalp.

"What time is it?" I ask.

"Almost time to go. I let you nap as long as I could. Getting to be a habit for you."

I start the sedan and pull into traffic. "Can't sleep."

"You sleep better than anyone else I know."

"Not at night."

"Why not?"

I just shrug and spray the windshield, the wipers creating an arc of dirt as the fluid sluices down the sides. "This town is filthy. Ten minutes in the car and we're covered in shit."

"It's been dirtier," Roland says. "The air used to be so filled with crap that I'd get black boogers when I was a kid." He takes another bite of his hotdog.

I wince. "Disgusting."

"I thought it was normal," adds Roland. "I'd get rocked in the snot box and bleed black and red. You want filthy, you should see a shirt full of bloody black boogers. This town has cleaned up a lot."

"Well, it's still filthy," I say, triggering the wiper fluid again. "I hate it." I dart down side streets and alleys strewn with discarded cardboard boxes and abandoned shopping carts to avoid the afternoon traffic on the highway. The dropping sun casts a red glare on each window as we pass.

"I like it," Roland says. "It's dirty in the right places."

"Yeah, well, you're a pig." I gesture at his hotdog. "And that's like eating a heart attack."

Roland grins, pops the rest of the hotdog in his mouth, and then takes a drag on his cigarette. "A dirty, smoky heart attack. Just how I like it. You can't live forever."

We reach the Sweet Tooth and drive by, peering into the parking lot and at the pedestrians walking nearby. I slowly circle the block, trying to see into each parked car as we pass.

"Just park, Reno," Roland says. "Jesus."

I ignore him. I learned a long time ago to trust my instincts. "Don't bother me. I'm doing my job."

"You're waking up from a goddamn nap is what you're doing."

I pull into an empty parking space and grab my Glock from underneath my seat, then pop open the glove compartment to retrieve a gift-wrapped box with a sloppy bow tied around the top.

"You better put out that cigarette before Cora catches you," I say as we step out of the sedan. "You know how she is."

"What's that?" Roland asks, nodding at the box.

"Birthday present for Victor."

"Shit—I forgot. Tell him it's from both us, 'kay?"

"Tell him yourself."

"He'll think I'm lying."

"You *are* lying." I pull out a key hung on a small chain around my neck and unlock the small door behind the shop. Roland follows me into Cora's kitchen, one hand waving the smoke from himself as he enters.

"At least let me sign the card," he says.

"No."

Victor is slouched in a chair by the mixing table and talking quietly into a phone. He waves at me and smiles. I smile back and pull up a stool, hiding the gift behind my back while Roland stalks into the front of the shop.

"Did the items get transferred?" Victor says into the phone. "And did he recognize the value? Uh, huh... Yeah, he knew the ratio… Yes. Okay, tell him the other items have already been moved." Victor compresses his lips into a thin line and shakes his head. "Remind him that market conditions determine the price, not me. This will be our last transaction anyway. Okay… Yeah… Tomorrow." He clicks off the phone.

I slide my gift across the stainless steel surface to him, the ribbon lazily trailing down one side of the box.

"What's this?"

"It's your birthday, right?"

Victor smiles warmly at me. "Why, yes it is. I didn't think anyone remembered." He shakes the box, puts it to his ear. "What could it be?" He even smells it, playing with me. Then he unwraps it carefully, slowly, and withdraws a silver letter opener, the slim blade winking in a ray from the setting sun shining through the glazed windows above the kitchen. "Thank you, Reno. That's very thoughtful." He leans forward and gives me a gentle kiss on the cheek. "It's beautiful, just like you."

I feel myself blush. "You're welcome, boss."

He leans back in his chair and smiles. "Well, it looks like I'm done for today. I just moved the last bits from the job. Tell Roland and Cora that we're going home early."

I march down the connecting hallway and into the front room. Cora is behind the register, counting up the till for the day. Roland stands near the front door, scanning the street through the front window.

"*Bella*, you must come by tomorrow," Cora says to me. "I have a new batch of persimmons. We can try it with the chocolate butter."

"Tomorrow morning?"

Cora nods, wisps of hair that had escaped her cooking

cap glowing in the light like a spiky halo. She tilts her head and looks more closely at me. "Are you feeling well, dear?"

I smile back and try to invigorate my reply. "Absolutely. Feeling good. Just a little tired today."

Cora leans toward me. "Roland says you have a gentlemen friend," she whispers conspiratorially.

"He does, huh? Well, he says lots of things. You can't always believe him."

Cora grabs both my hands. "Roland says he surfs in the ocean. I want to meet him."

"You two had quite a chat," I laugh. "He's not my boyfriend. Turns out I don't know him that well."

"Roland said you like him."

"Victor wants to go home early. Are you ready?"

"Yes, dear."

Cora and Victor chat happily all the way home, with Roland chiming in on every topic. Her rose perfume fills the cabin and I feel relaxed and happy. It's always my favorite time of day, listening to them talk and laugh.

I don't have to be quite so careful when we're in this sedan. At my insistence, Victor agreed to install Lexan shielding throughout the car. The powerful engine and performance tires nicely balance the two-plus tons of weight. I like the mix of heft and power. Although slower with the Lexan panels, it handles well and I feel safe in it.

I wonder if Jack is still pissed. Probably. I guess I don't blame him, but it wasn't like he was completely honest with me either. I'll try to talk to him tonight, I promise myself.

We reach Victor's villa, his gate opening to several guards and my Ducati. The motorcycle's missing the faring and scuffed, but with four valves and more than a hundred horsepower, it's my favorite thing in the world.

My good mood evaporates when Victor pulls me aside and hands me a large envelope. "This is Carter's cut, including his crew's. I told him you would drop it off and figure out the details of the caviar job."

I take the envelope and shake my head. "We shouldn't do it."

Victor squints at me. "We've covered this. It's not like I have a choice, do I? Just a couple more weeks, I promise. And why are you so concerned about this job?"

I hesitate. I've made too many promises, I think. Promises to not interrupt Zhukov's operations, promises to Gartello not to tell Victor, too many promises. A shiver of fear shoots through me as I remember Zhukov's threats. *I devour my enemies like lions eat.* I look helplessly at Victor. "I just don't have a good feeling about it."

Victor narrows his eyes. "So figure it out. Make sure he isn't going to screw it up."

Resigned, I nod. "Okay." Maybe I *could* pull it off. If Zhukov doesn't connect the heist to Victor, if Carter's connections hold up, if they can move the caviar without the Russians getting word… but that's too many fucking "ifs" for my liking.

After ensuring that Victor and Cora are secure, I swing my leg over the Ducati and crank it alive. As it warms up, Roland eases the sedan out of the driveway. He stops and rolls the window down as he pulls up alongside me. "See you here tomorrow morning?"

"Yeah."

Roland pauses. "What's up with you?"

"Gotta see Carter."

"Oh. Want me to come along?"

I almost say yes, but shake my head instead. "No, I'm fine. Go home and kiss Angela for me."

"Sorry about earlier," he says, surprising me. Roland is not famous for his apologies. "I was just joking, you know, about your sex life. I just want you to have somebody special in your life, like I have Angela. I think you'd be happier."

"Don't worry about it," I say, still a little shocked.

"No, I mean it. I was an asshole." He drums the steering wheel—a little embarrassed, I think. "Hey, Zhukov reached out to me. Wants me to come aboard."

"What did you say?"

"What do you think I said? I told him he only had three brain cells, and two of them were busy holding his asshole shut."

"Classy."

"He repeated it to his crew and they all laughed. I kind of warmed up to him after that. Kick Carter in the balls for me."

A few moments later I'm streaking up the highway, splitting traffic and ignoring the stop signs, the quick lightness of the Ducati a nice contrast to the sedan. If Zhukov is actively recruiting both Roland and me, does that mean that he's preparing for the transition? Looking to weaken Victor further? I'm worried, but the evening's cool air perks me up, and by the time I arrive in the industrial section of town, I'm ready for Carter.

He lives in an old graffiti-covered warehouse. A rusted fence topped with barbed wire lines the perimeter. Bits of trash stick in the barbs and twirl in the wind. I park the Ducati in the gutter and pick my way through a mound of asphalt shingles and hammer on the steel door. After a long delay, I hear him throw the bolt and he flings the door open.

He smirks at me. "I knew it was just a matter of time before we fucked."

"You live in a garbage dump, do you know that?"

"If you had my medical bills you'd live in a dump too."

I slap the envelope of cash into his hand. "Well, this should help then. Here's your cut from the jewelry job."

He nods. "Very nice."

"You going to invite me in?"

"You going to show me your panties?"

"So you could wear them yourself?"

"Maybe." He waves me in. Lined up on a shelf along one wall are jars filled with formaldehyde and various specimens. I peer at them closer. Some look like animals, fetuses of some sort, while others could be human organs.

"What the hell is this shit?" I ask.

"None of your business, princess. What do you want?"

"Victor wants me to go over the caviar job."

"You just show up on time—that's all you need to know. It's my job."

"No, it's *our* job."

"Last I checked, you didn't want to be part of it."

"You forced him into it." I shake my head in disgust. "Why don't you just leave him alone? It's shitty to threaten an old man with jail time."

His smirk has been growing as I talk, and he finally bursts into laughter. "You really don't know anything!" He shakes his head and wipes his eyes. "God, you're a piece of work. Wait here a minute."

Carter disappears through a metal door at the back of what I suppose is his living room. I look around and notice a cage near a dirty window. It contains a tattered parrot, its blue and yellow feathers dull and waxy. I wonder if it's real. As I draw near, the musty smell of dried bird droppings fill my nose. A filthy black sheet lies crumpled on the ground below the cage. The parrot's eyes are shut and I think it must be dead. But when I tap on the cage, its eyes snap open and it lets out a horrible scream, its black tongue emerging from its beak like a worm.

"Stop it, Carter! Stop it!" the parrot screeches in a sad, pitiful voice. It bounces up and down in its cage. "Stop it, Carter! Stop it!"

Breathing heavily, I stare at the bird, unsure what to do. Then Carter flings open the door. Holding a VHS tape in one hand, he angrily stamps over to the cage. With one hand he picks up the black sheet and throws it over the screaming parrot. "Shut the fuck up, asshole!" he yells.

He shoves the tape into my hands, takes off his shoe, and beats the covered cage with it. "Go to sleep!" he shouts. He throws the shoe onto the ground and limps over to a couch listing in front of a TV propped on a cardboard box. "Come here," he says to me.

I just stand there.

"You deaf?" he asks irritably.

"What's wrong with that thing?"

"Just ignore it. Used to belong to my mother." He points to a VCR sitting on the floor near the TV. "Pop in that tape and take a load off."

I look down at him. "I'm not sitting next to you."

"Suit yourself."

I slide the tape into the machine and hear it whir to life.

Carter picks up his remote. "So you think I'm blackmailing Victor, huh? Picking on an old man?"

"Yes."

"Well, I'm not. Not really."

"You're a liar."

"Yes," he says brightly, "but not about this. Believe it or not, Victor is trying to do you a favor—you're just too stupid to see it."

"What the hell are you talking about?"

He presses the play button and smirks at me.

A grainy surveillance tape flashes onto the television screen. It takes a moment to make out the dark shape of a sedan parked almost directly in front of the camera. A sign across the street flickers SWAN GALLERY in neon.

Suddenly a chill fills me. I know that name. "What's this?"

"Just wait," Carter says. "It gets better. Much better."

The windows of the sedan, opaque from the darkness and low fidelity of the recording, abruptly bloom with light as the doors open and the interior dome light goes on. What looks like a young woman steps out of the car and then turns to look directly into the camera as she absently tucks a cross under her shirt. Carter pauses the tape, causing the image to roll, distorted and stretched, across the television screen before stabilizing.

"Look familiar?" Carter asks. "Recognize her from anywhere?"

I see my own face staring back at me. "Where did you get this?"

He smiles. "World's a funny place. This old guy across the street is selling boutique bonsai. He installs a security camera, and then for some reason you park there at… let's see." He leans forward and squints. "At three in the morning. Hmmm, I wonder what you're doing?" Carter laughs as a coldness forms in my heart. He presses the play button and the tape rolls forward.

I watch myself lug two red cans of kerosene from the trunk and waddle awkwardly across the street. I remember it now. An arson fraud. The owner of the gallery replaced his paintings with inexpensive canvas imitations and had us torch the place. Victor kept the paintings for fence, and the gallery picked up the insurance money for the paintings and building. We had done several arson jobs before, and this one had been nothing out of the ordinary. Until now.

Carter presses fast-forward, and the tape leaps ahead until the building erupts with a bright blaze of light. Carter hits the play button again and captures a figure running full-speed toward the camera, cradling a can in each arm. "You always had a grace about you. I'll give you that much. Stupid as a sack of hammers sometimes, but graceful about it."

I see myself jump in the driver's seat after dumping the empty cans of kerosene into the trunk. The building is already burning as my sedan pulls away.

Carter ejects the tape and holds it in front of me. "I'm actually grateful, Reno. Without you, Victor and I wouldn't be partners. You should have seen his face when I showed him this. Arson is a serious crime, you know." He shakes his head, chuckling. "You must know that he's very fond of you. While I don't exactly share those feelings, out of respect for our new partnership I agreed to withhold this tape. Victor has been grateful ever since."

Carter's voice dimly reaches me. I dully look at the black

tape cassette in his hands. All this time… "Shut up!" I snap at Carter with tears in my eyes.

Carter stands up and closes to within inches of my face. I can smell a rancid fish odor oozing from him. "Little Miss Kickass suddenly wishing she had been nicer to old Carter, huh? Not too late for a thank-you blowjob."

"Shut up!" I say again, blood roaring in my ears.

"Don't tell me to shut up just because you don't like the truth," he spits. "You walk around like your shit doesn't stink, and now you find out that you're the turd in the bowl. It's your turn to shut up."

For one brief moment I think about pulling the switchblade from my boot and gutting him. He might have sensed it too, because he takes a step back. But then I remember Victor's admonishment to just sit tight. Time is on our side. Screw Carter. He'll get a blade to the gut soon enough.

"Do you ever deal straight with anybody?" I ask. "Or do you always just creep around in your lies? Do you have any actual friends?"

Carter's smirk is back. "Maybe if you and I could be friends, this tape and all my copies could just disappear. You could make life a whole lot easier for Victor."

"Fuck you, Carter."

He smiles. "Now we're talking. You could be my extra-special fuck buddy."

I walk toward the door.

"If you loved Victor as much as he loves you," he shouts after me, "you would do whatever I say!"

July 7, 1986, 6:53 P.M.

"Just mistakes I've made."

I slam the door behind me and stand in the cool night air wiping my eyes and softly cursing to myself. All this time, we've been forced to endure Carter because of me. Victor's been groveling to that monster to protect me, not himself.

I start the Ducati, twist the throttle, and fly up the street, splitting traffic. Furious with Carter and myself, I hit the freeway ramp in top gear, streaking through the night. All of Carter's blackmail because of my mistake.

After several miles, I calm down and take the next exit, circling back into the city. Just be patient, I tell myself. The statute of limitations runs out in a couple weeks. After that, Carter can go to hell. *Will* go to hell. Almost by reflex, I find myself rocking my bike on its kickstand outside the Last Call.

The music fills me like it always does, and I drift on its rhythm, trying to empty my mind. Jack's usual high-tempo mix lets me work up a sweat, and before long the anger and memories of Carter fade. I break for a few gulps of water but otherwise dance for hours, trying to exhaust myself and maybe get in a few hours of sleep before dawn.

Jack doesn't seem to be working tonight. I don't know

what I'd say to him anyway. I feel stupid for how I had acted about Carmen. As the bar closes and the last customers are leaving, the soft notes from a piano mingle with the scrape and clatter of the chairs being stacked. I peer across the dance floor and see Jack seated at the battered old piano with his back to me.

Jack plays slowly, almost caressing the keys. I don't recognize the song, but it sounds classical to me. The bartender stops too, and listens to the soft echoes of the composition filling the room. I can actually feel the live piano music so much better than the house mix that normally blasts from the speakers. When Jack finally stops twenty minutes later, I clap.

He turns around, surprised. "How long have you been sitting there?"

I shrug. "Long enough."

Jack gets up from the piano and walks over with a shy smile. I enjoy watching his easy athletic stroll.

"You know what?" he says. "I talk too much." Before I can respond, he leans over and kisses me on the mouth.

I pull away, my old instincts as strong as ever, but then I kiss him back. He tastes like an intoxicating mix of the ocean and smoke and sweat.

He pulls away and I put my hand on his heart. "Your heartbeat has picked up a bit."

He puts his hand on my chest, high enough to avoid a slap. "Yours too." He leans into me again and we kiss again. "You're beautiful," he says.

"Maybe you don't talk too much," I say, a little flustered. "I thought you were mad at me."

"Yeah, I was mad, but I'm guilty of the exact same shit. I wasn't exactly straight with you either." He's standing so close to me that I can feel his warmth. "I really like you, and I'm glad you came over tonight."

I lean in and kiss him.

In one motion he wraps his arms around me and lifts me off my feet. We kiss again as he carries me across the dance floor. He kicks open a door near the back, and we enter what must be his bedroom. He swings the door shut with another kick and we fall onto the bed.

The red neon sign of Last Call flashes through the windows as Jack slips his hand under my blouse. His hands are hot on my body and I arch my back into him. We kiss and I ache for him, my nipples pushing at the fabric of my bra. His kisses run down my neck as his hands unbutton my blouse. He licks my breast and I moan. Then he tugs down my jeans. I grind into him, pulling him tight, clawing the clothes from his wiry, muscular surfer's body.

My hands cup his ass as I hungrily draw him into me. We rock together, our bodies melding into one. My body quivers as we both gasp from a climax that fills me with a flash of heat and then a warm melting. We lie there for a while, holding each other.

Soon Jack's deep regular breaths lull me into a trance, and I feel myself drifting off. In his arms, I feel a sense of bliss and peace that is unlike anything I've ever felt before. Maybe that asshole Roland was right.

I wake in the morning, sunlight bouncing off what looks like parts from a million clocks or maybe old stereos hanging on the walls and stacked on shelves. It's a little surprising, and hard to identify what they used to belong to. What's even more surprising is how rested I feel. I slept through the night without waking once, for the first time in so long. I look over at Jack and kiss his ear.

Jack opens his eyes. "Hey…" he murmurs.

We kiss and I roll onto him, reveling in the touch of his chest against mine. Jack's hands rest on my hips as I rock into him. A pulse of electricity jolts through me as Jack squeezes my breasts, pressing them upward with his palms. We find a rhythm, and I groan. He pulls me closer, and I feel a pressure build and build and then burst into an orgasm.

I collapse on him, and we lie there in a lazy haze as Jack gently traces his finger along my back, lightly caressing the round welts shaped like dimes. "What happened to you?" he asks. The alarm in his voice pulls me back into the moment. For a brief moment I see myself as he must: my skin glowing bronze in the morning sun, but a quilt of scars marring my back. A fading bruise down my left side looks like a thundercloud tattoo, and a discolored notch interrupts the smooth curve of my left ear.

"All these scars…" His finger traces a puckered white scar near my hip.

"Just mistakes I've made." I roll off the bed, slip on my panties, and grab what looks like some sort of timer or maybe a clock. "What's this?" I ask, hoping to change the topic.

Jack shrugs. "That's a Radionics control box keypad, specifically for the Omega alarm, model number D6112. You might ask why I have a bunch of disassembled alarms in my bedroom, and I would tell you that a certain Russian warehouse uses that exact model to secure their doors."

"So Carmen convinced you to work on Carter's caviar job?" I ask. "Thought you weren't a fan."

"Don't always have a choice." He looks at me evenly, and I wonder what he's thinking.

"I thought you and Carmen were partners," I say, and his face reddens. "Don't you have a say?"

Jack pulls me back into his bed. "We're not getting along very well right now. She just got out, and she's making up for lost time, and I'm just done with that life. I agreed to help on this job, but only if we followed my plan and used no guns."

That feeling of dread floods back into me. I should never have agreed to anything with Zhukov. Ripping off crazy Russians while unarmed is prohibited by good sense and any desire to live a long life. Getting involved with Jack when he's already involved with Carmen is also not smart.

"You shouldn't get involved," I say. Good advice for both of us.

"Too late." He kisses the back of my neck and I shiver. "Why are you so opposed to this?"

I'm no good at secrets, not really. And I already lied to Jack once and don't want to do it again. "Look, it's complicated. Victor is wrapping up his operations, and we don't want any trouble with Zhukov."

"I'm with you. But this thing is already rolling, and Carter didn't make it sound like you had much choice. He calls the shots for Victor, doesn't he?"

"Not for long." I pick up a loose alarm part and twirl it in my hand. "I told Zhukov we wouldn't touch his operations in exchange for a truce. If we get caught breaking the truce, he has enough men to hunt us all down."

With that Jack sits up a little straighter and his eyes narrow. "So why is Victor going along with this?"

"He doesn't know about the truce."

Jack shakes his head. "So stay out of it. We can handle it without you."

"Won't matter. He'll know we're involved just because of Carter's involvement."

"So we won't get caught," Jack says and kisses me again.

July 9, 1986, 10:19 A.M.

"I thought we could keep each other safe."

"And you kissed him?" Cora asks in a hushed voice, her hands deftly rolling the chocolate-dipped truffles into shaved coffee beans.

I carefully dip another ball of raspberry ganache into her double boiler of tempered chocolate. "Well, he kissed me first, actually."

"That's even better," Cora says.

I pull the ganache from the chocolate with my fingers and then hand it to Cora, who rolls it in the coffee beans. "Delicious," I say, licking my fingers.

"My chocolate or Jack's kiss?" Cora teases.

"Both," I say and we giggle. "I had a good sleep too."

"You need more sleep," Cora chides. "Go to bed earlier."

"It doesn't matter when I go to bed."

Cora frowns. "What's wrong that you can't sleep?"

I wash my hands and dip another ganache into the warm chocolate. "I don't know."

But I *do* know. The same feelings of dread, like I'm about to fall off a tightrope strung between two skyscrapers. I worry about Cora, Victor, myself… I think about the tape and feel sick to my stomach again. All of the grief that Carter's caused because of my stupid mistake…

We work in silence for a while until the back door swings open. I recognize Roland's tread down the hallway, his big shoes creaking the floor in his usual bouncy cadence.

"Hello, ladies!" he bellows as he enters the kitchen. "Hmmm, I smell chocolate." He reaches for a cooling truffle only to be slapped away by Cora.

"Wash your hands!"

He gives her a hurt look. "My hands are clean! I washed them this morning."

Cora points to the sink. "Go. Don't argue with old women."

Roland shakes his head and rinses his hand at the sink, then walks over to me. "Carter's in the back with Victor," he whispers. "They want you."

I kiss Cora on the cheek and towel off my hands. "I'll be right back."

"Okay, dear." Cora nods to Roland. "You should always wash your hands."

"I told you they were clean. I have very clean hands, Cora."

I leave them to their bickering, walk to the back room, and poke my head through the doorway. "Yeah, boss?"

"I want to go over the caviar job," Victor says.

"Neither of you needs to worry about a damn thing," Carter says. He opens a packet of sugar and pours it down his throat. "I've got Chopek, and he gets things done. Nothing to worry about."

Victor considers that for a moment. "He's not a good choice."

Carter pulls his inhaler from his coat and sucks on it. "He's my ticket into the docks." He rips open another sugar packet and offers it to Victor. "Want some?"

Victor declines with a wave of his hand.

Carter dumps the sugar down his throat and reaches for another. "It'll work fine, just like last time. Carmen knows what she has to do. So does Chopek." He stands up and nods to me. "Don't be late."

He struts from the room and slams the door behind him. Victor props his reading glasses on his head and peers at me. "What?"

I shrug. "Nothing."

"Nothing? You always get that face when there's something. I don't like it when you hold back."

"I guess I learned that from you."

He squints at me. "What does that mean?"

"Nothing."

He tosses his glasses onto the table. "Okay, spit it out."

"I know."

He smiles. "And if you tell me, we'll both know."

"I saw the tape," I say quietly. "I know how Carter is blackmailing you."

"Reno—"

"You don't need to protect me," I interrupt. "I can take care of this myself." I feel tears well up in my eyes, which just makes me angrier. "I'll kill him and go back to Colombia. You won't have to worry about me or him."

"Reno—" he begins again, a tired smile on his face.

"I'm supposed to protect you!" I say. "Not the other way around! The last five years, all this shit with Carter, just over me? Why didn't you tell me? I could have left, I could have taken care of it! I should have known!" I realize that I'm shouting at the top of my lungs and stop to regain my composure. The chatter from the kitchen has gone dead silent. "Why didn't you tell me?" I ask softly.

"Because I knew you would act like this."

I wipe my nose and glare at him.

Victor stands up, places both hands on my shoulders, and looks into my eyes. "You're special to me. I couldn't stand it if you left. And yes, Carter knew that and used it against me. But it was worth it to me."

"I'm supposed to keep you safe, not cause more problems."

"I thought we could keep each other safe."

I can see the concern and hurt in his eyes. "You should have told me," I whisper.

He takes a deep breath. "You sound like Gartello. And maybe you're both right. But the statute runs out in a couple of weeks, and then it will be our turn."

"Will you do something for me?"

He nods.

"Don't do the caviar job. Delay it somehow."

A flash of annoyance twists his face.

"What is with you about this job?" he says. "We've talked about this over and over. Carter isn't bluffing about the tape, and you haven't exactly endeared yourself to him."

I take a breath, reluctant to confess my agreement with Gartello and Zhukov, but I don't see any other choice. "I promised Zhukov that we'd leave him alone if he did the same. If he finds out we stole the caviar, he'll come down on us hard and we don't have the manpower. We only have Oscar and his crew. They wouldn't last a day."

Victor's face hardens into the mask of determination and

anger that I had once learned to fear. In the old days it meant serious trouble.

"Now who's keeping secrets, Reno!" He sweeps the papers from the table and his glasses clatter against the hard tile. "What the hell were you thinking, going behind my back like that?"

I don't say anything.

He glares at me and then his expression changes into something impossible to read. "The old man," he says to himself. "So it's that way, is it? Gartello got you to do this? Run some sort of deal so old soft Victor isn't destroyed? You don't think I can handle Zhukov?"

"It's just a truce."

He wipes his mouth and bends over to pick up his glasses with a tired groan. "We're doing the caviar job."

"I gave my word that we wouldn't."

"But it was *my* word on this, not yours," Victor snaps. "You don't speak for me, no matter what Gartello thinks. Just do as I ask and don't try to fix things you can't fix. Do the job and don't provoke Carter. Don't talk to Zhukov again. Easy directions. You follow me?"

I nod.

Victor examines his glasses. A spider web of fractures has ruined the left lens and he tosses the glasses onto the table. He rubs his face and seems to deflate with a long, weary sigh.

"Reno," he says softly, "in my heart, you're my daughter. I will always love you as family. But lies and secrets will tear us apart." He wipes his eyes and swallows. "We need to trust each other."

Tears burn my eyes. Victor doesn't think I trust him. I feel ashamed. I trust him more than anyone in my life. I squeeze my eyes shut and hug him as hard as I can, which I think surprises him. I can't remember the last time we hugged. After a brief pause he hugs me back and my heart unclenches.

"I'm sorry," I say.

"Me too."

"So what do we do now?"

"Do the job," he says, "and then we'll give it all away to Gartello. If he wants to work with Zhukov, that's his decision."

He gives me a smile but I'm filled with dread. I think of Zhukov and his dead eyes. *I devour my enemies like lions eat.*

July 10, 1986, 2:19 A.M.

"You ever try to outsmart a bullet?"

Rain sluices between the wiper blades and blurs the lights of passing cars as Jack pilots the diesel truck toward the harbor. He works through the gears, winding up the diesel, lugging it down into the next gear and back up again. Carmen and I sit in the back of the cab. I can feel the frost coming from her. A flash of lightning illuminates the road for an instant before returning to a watery haze.

"The guy we're picking up might be a bit psycho," I say.

"So I hear," Jack grunts. ""How can you be a *bit* psycho? Isn't that like being a little bit pregnant?"

"We need him to get into the docks. He's fixed the customs agent. He's probably carrying a gun though."

Jack frowns and jams the truck into a lower gear, slowing down for a stop sign. "Guns are for the stupid."

"You ever try to outsmart a bullet, Jack?" Carmen says.

"That's the whole point," he says. "No guns mean we're more careful, we're thinking, and we're scared. Those are all good things. If you're carrying a piece, you've knocked off fifty points from your IQ. If things don't look good enough to do it unarmed, don't do it."

"And if something unexpected happens?" I say.

"Then it wasn't planned right," he says. "It's not too late to turn around, you know."

Carmen sucks her teeth. "Yeah, that's true. But do you really want to piss off Carter?"

"Happily." After a moment, Jack sighs. "So how psycho is this Chopek guy?" he asks me.

"I think even Carter's scared of him," I say.

Jack groans. "Great."

"You going to convince Chopek to ditch his gun too?" I ask.

"You sure he's carrying?"

"Yeah, guys like him always carry. No IQ points to lose."

A few moments later, Jack eases the rig into the parking lot of a small grocery store and lets it idle. A car nestled near the back alley flashes its lights.

"That's him," I say.

"When I grab him, you pull the gun," Jack says to me, perfectly calm like he's ordering waffles.

"I'm not crazy about that idea," Carmen says. "Reno?"

"Well, I did agree to leave my gun behind," I say, still debating whether it was a small mistake or a giant one. "But yeah, I'm not crazy about it either."

Jack flashes the semi's lights. The car door opens and Ivan Chopek, dressed in a grubby jumpsuit, dashes through the light rain toward the truck.

"Just leave him alone," Carmen says.

"Grab his legs when you get a chance," Jack tells me.

"You're late," Chopek complains as he opens the cab door.

"Yeah, sorry about that," Jack says as he extends his hand to pull Chopek into the cab. "Weather held us up." As their hands clasp, Jack jerks him hard across the passenger seat. Surprised, Chopek twists and falls onto the floorboard.

Jack uses both hands to grab the back of Chopek's neck and press him hard to the floor. I slide between the seats and press my knees into Chopek's back.

Chopek claws at Jack and pushes up to his knees, tossing me backward. An elbow crashes into my ear. Chopek is wheezing now, a high whine pushing through his gritted teeth. Or maybe it's my ear, I don't really know. I just struggle to pin his thrashing legs. Another flailing elbow hits me in the neck.

"We're not going to hurt you," Jack yells at him. "Just relax!"

Chopek finally goes limp. "If you kill me, Carter hunt you down," he pants.

"We're not going to kill you, Ivan," Jack replies. "Just instituting a new policy. You just get us through customs, no need for a gun."

I feel Chopek relax.

"No guns?" Chopek says.

"We're doing it Jack's way," Carmen says. "He's increasing your IQ."

"He's idiot," Chopek gasps.

Carmen erupts with a peal of laughter.

"No gun," Jack says. "Either that, or the deal's off."

Breathing heavily, Chopek considers this for a moment. "Okay, no gun."

"Good," Jack grunts. "Where's your piece?"

"Front pocket."

I fish around and pull the revolver from Chopek's pocket.

I hand it to Jack, who releases Chopek's neck and tucks the gun in the door-side pocket.

I slide into the backseat with Carmen while Chopek climbs up to the passenger side of the front seat. We all catch our breaths for a moment as I rub my ear, which is bleeding, and then Jack puts the truck into gear.

Jack looks back at me and says, "You okay?"

I nod and Jack continues driving toward the harbor. When we cross the next bridge, Jack flings the pistol into the water as Chopek stares sullenly out the window.

Twenty minutes later, Jack steers the rig into the harbor entrance and brakes for a uniformed guard at the gate. He rolls down his window, and Chopek leans over. "*Eto dlya vas i vashey sem'i, s nashimi spasibo*," he says to the guard.

Chopek hands the man an envelope. I assume it's cash, but who knows. It could be drugs. Or both. The guard waves us through and just like that we're in customs.

Jack hugs the edge of the harbor, following the dock to a collection of rundown warehouses that are distant from the central hub. In a few hours, the dawn will bring a caravan of container trucks, but it's quiet for now.

We stop near the rear door of a warehouse that's clad in rusty tin. One pale yellow bulb glows above a dented roll-up door, the new alarm box bolted next to it a stark contrast to the surrounding decay.

I peer at the surrounding buildings. A maze of warehouses and alleys crisscross the pier— making it impossible to see any unfriendlies until they're right on top of us. I check my watch. 2:57 A.M.

"Carter said he'd meet us here," Carmen says.

Just then a tiny beam of light winks on and off from the shadows of the warehouse.

"That's got to be him," I say.

Jack flicks the truck lights on and off. The rain has stopped, but fog swirls in the beams. Carter steps into the pale yellow light near the door and waves us over.

Carter sucks a blast from his silver canister. "The Russians cleared out a couple hours ago," he says. "We have until daybreak." He pats his police radio on his hip. "I'll know if Jack fucks up the security."

I look over at Chopek, who's nursing a growing bruise on his cheek. His eyes narrow. "He won't," I say tightly. "Do your thing, Jack."

Without a word, Jack spins on his heels and strides back to the truck. He comes back with a duffle bag, squats below the alarm box, and pulls out a small device with a neatly soldered EPROM chip dangling from an interface ribbon. With a small tape measure he marks a couple points on the panel, and then grabs a hand drill from his bag.

The drill sounds loud in the night, but I just breathe deeper and try to ignore the jitters creeping up my spine. Jack threads some sort of clips through the holes he's made in the case, and then attaches the EPROM chip onto the leads, and then finally attaches some sort of monitor that Carmen has lugged out from the truck. A few moments later, he's scrolling through a series of characters and numbers. They make no sense to me, but Jack looks satisfied and almost happy.

Chopek walks over. "I make your ear bloody," he says, his eyes now squinted with amusement.

The entire left side of my head is throbbing from his elbows.

Jack keeps scrolling through the symbols, I think looking for the embedded alphanumeric codes that are mapped to the entrance code. Or something like that. He told me earlier, but I honestly couldn't follow him that well. It looks like a mess so far.

"The whole fucking thing might be encrypted," he murmurs to himself. "Even the upper registers?" Blisters of sweat rise on the back of his neck.

"Speed it up," Carter hisses.

Jack's eyes don't leave the screen as symbols scroll by in a cascade of gibberish.

"Jack?" Carter says. "We don't have all fucking night." He turns to Carmen. "You said he had this."

"Shut up," Jack says, his eyes still fixed on the screen. "Okay, we're good," he says a moment later.

"Good?" Carter asks. "How good?"

Jack gives me a wink, walks over to the keypad, and punches in a series of numbers. The blinking red LED switches to a steady green glow, and the door latch clacks open.

"That good," Jack says.

Carter bends down and grabs the roll-up door handle. A silver gleam from a revolver stuffed in the back of his waistband catches my eye. Carter is probably more unstable than Chopek, and I briefly think about taking his gun too. Fuck it. His IQ will never go up.

The door rattles open to reveal a large cargo container gleaming in the stark warehouse lighting. Carter swings open the container doors. Grins fill their faces as they take in the neatly stacked pallets of caviar, but I just want to have this done as quickly as possible. *Time to rob the robbers*. If Zhukov finds out that I broke my promise…

"I'll guide you in," I say to Jack. "Let's go."

Jack jumps into the cab and restarts the rig. The big diesel rumbles a shiver through my feet as Jack disengages the clutch and reverses into the warehouse. The diesel engine echoes in the confined space of the building and blasts out fat black tendrils of exhaust. I briefly wonder about carbon monoxide fumes, but we won't be here much longer than the few minutes it will take to latch the container and cable it to the cab.

Carter keeps watch just outside the entrance. Chopek drifts over to him, and the two men mutter to each other in low voices.

Jack turns off the engine and Carmen starts attaching the cables and brake lines. As he swings down from the cab to help, I notice a man standing motionless at the back of the warehouse next to a slightly ajar small door. I don't know how long he's been standing there. Probably not very long.

His rumpled clothing and tousled hair indicate that he probably just woke up. He shifts slightly when he sees me looking at him. Now I notice the large pistol in the holster at his side. I take a short breath and smile at him.

"Hey, how you doing?" I call out. I smile with what I hope is a carefree, "gee, glad to see you" look but as I walk over I see suspicion on his face. There's another alarm box mounted on the wall right next to him. I hope he hasn't triggered it. I silently curse Carter. Nobody is supposed to be here.

"*Golnak skazal utrom, ne seychas,*" he says.

I don't know how to answer that.

He frowns and repeats himself in English: "Golnak said in morning, not now."

I keep my eyes from trailing to the gun. Look relaxed, I tell myself. Just doing business as usual.

"Yeah, we're moving early." I shrug. "Zhukov wants it done now, what can you do?"

His hand rests on the gun, but doesn't move, which I think is a very good sign. I see a pack of cigarettes in his breast pocket and smile at him again. "Got a smoke?" I don't even smoke, but I'm desperate to keep him occupied until I can figure something out.

He hesitates, but then pulls the cigarettes from his shirt pocket and offers me one. He lights mine and then his. I put the cigarette to my mouth, but I'm afraid I'll cough if I inhale.

We both look across the warehouse floor. Carmen falters just a second when she gazes over at us. But then she smoothly grabs an air cable, snakes it back to the hitch, and yells "Hey, give me a hand, okay?" at me.

"Be right back," I say and try to saunter over to the truck.

"Who the hell is that?" Jack whispers.

"You tell me," I reply. "I think I calmed him down, but he's got a gun and I bet he calls somebody soon."

Jack walks to the front of the trailer. "We got company," he says to Chopek. "Near the back."

Chopek takes a few steps to his left and curses under his breath.

"Why don't you just take his gun too, Jack?" Carmen whispers scornfully.

"Just relax," Jack says. "I'll handle it."

Carter pokes his head in the door. "What the fuck are you idiots doing? Hook this pig up and let's go. Come on!"

Chopek deftly pulls the revolver from Carter's waistband and promptly marches across the garage bay, the gun casually draped at his side opposite the guard. He waves his free hand at the guard and says, "*Vy ne vozrazhayete, pomogaya nam?*"

It sounds cheerful. The guard looks like he's considering something.

Still moving forward, Chopek simply extends his arm from his side and yanks the trigger before the guard can react. The gunshot sharply echoes off the tin roof and walls. The man staggers back, hand fumbling at his holster. Chopek fires twice more. The guard slumps against the floor, his shattered skull banging against the wall.

"Goddammit!" Carter curses. "Fucking jackass! Get in the truck—we have to move right now."

Chopek still holds the gun outstretched.

"What the fuck are you doing?" I yell. "We could've handled him. Jesus!"

"He see my face," Chopek spits. "That is for me death sentence."

"You asshole."

Chopek waves his revolver at me. "I save lives. If Zhukov finds out, he kills us all."

He has a point there.

Jack runs up and puts his hand on my shoulder. "We'll settle this later. We gotta go."

Carter is frantically waving us over. "Come on! Start this truck. We gotta go! Units are rolling our way!" His police radio is crackling with terse chatter.

"We'll talk about this later!" Jack yells at Chopek.

Chopek stares at Jack with hooded eyes, but then nods. "*Da*, we go." He waves his revolver at Jack. "Drag him in truck. Maybe Zhukov think him thief."

"Are you out of your fucking mind?" I ask. "Bring him with us? That won't fool Zhukov. There's blood everywhere. Jesus!"

Chopek's face goes slack.

"Just drag him into that back room, okay?" Jack says. "We don't have time for this. I'll grab the truck."

Chopek looks at me one more time, but then kneels and grabs the guard under one arm. "You take other," he says. His heels leave bloody streaks on the concrete.

"Poppa?"

A little girl stands in the ruined doorway. She clutches a raggedy teddy bear in her arms. Her sleepy eyes blink in the harsh light of the garage.

"Hi, honey," I say softly. "You shouldn't be up. It's late. Go back to bed."

She just stares at me. She can't be older than three.

Chopek drops the guard's arm and walks toward the girl with the revolver behind his back. "You should not have come down here."

I see Chopek's thumb pull back the hammer. Horrified and ashamed, I drop my eyes to the ground. I can't bear to watch. Then I see the guard's gun, still in its holster.

Chopek swings the revolver toward the little girl.

"Stop!"

Chopek slowly looks over his shoulder. He freezes when he sees me holding the dead man's pistol.

"Don't do it," I snarl.

Chopek's eyes narrow. "You make big mistake."

Carter's radio chirps again. "Come on! Patrol is on the way! Quit fucking around!"

Tears run down the little girl's face. She hugs her teddy bear. "You're not going to do this," I say. "Put the fucking gun down right now."

"Zhukov kill all of us." He turns away from me and back to the little girl.

"Don't," I say flatly.

I hear the thin distant wail of a siren.

Chopek swings the gun up to the little girl's head.

I pull the trigger. Smoke curls around my face as Chopek rises up on his toes, half spun around from the impact. A look of surprise and pain twists his lips into a rictus smile. Then he falls heavily, Carter's service revolver clattering across the floor to my feet.

The little girl is crying, her face pressed into her teddy bear.

I hear the screech of tires outside and the wail of sirens fills the bay. Jack and Carmen run toward me, their faces crinkled with panic. Carter follows behind, wheezing.

Jack grabs my hand. "Out back!" he says.

My head clears a little. I yank my hand free and pull the little girl to the side. "Wait for the men with badges, okay?" She nods and buries her face back into her teddy bear.

Jack grabs my hand again and pulls me away. We race through the back door and down a shabby hallway as Carter wheezes and stumbles behind us.

Carmen, Jack, and I pass one small room and then the hallway ends in a fire door. Jack kicks it open and we burst into what looks like the back warehouse, the same one where Carter ostensibly serves as a moonlighting guard. Stacks of palleted electronic gear rise to the ceiling. Heavy padlocks secure the roll-up doors. A series of windows high up on the wharf-side wall glow from the pearl moonlight and a briny night breeze blows off the water through some broken panes of glass high above.

"Which way?" Jack says, breathing heavily.

"Climb," I reply, pointing up to the skylights. "Get to those windows."

I scrabble up a stack of pallets by the windows. Pausing to catch my breath, I look down to see Carter grab Carmen by the back of the neck.

"My gun," he gasps at her. "Who has my fucking gun?" She kicks at him, but then loses her grip and they both fall to the ground. K-9 dogs bark in the near distance, and a shiver of fear runs through me.

To my horror, Jack starts to climb back down the pallets, but the piercing beams of flashlights and the squeak of broken hinges send him scrambling back to me as the police enter with drawn guns.

We watch from atop the pallets as troopers tackle Carter and Carmen. Jack winces as a cop pins Carmen with a knee to her back and yanks her arm up behind her. Carter goes prone, spread-eagled with hands facing up. "I'm a federal agent," I hear him say. "My name is Carter Hansen. You can find identification in my coat pocket."

A burly deputy quickly searches him, pulling out his inhaler, his badge, and a jumble of keys and tiny vodka bottles. The cop shrugs, grabs Carter's hand, and pulls him up.

"I was just doing a little moonlighting when I heard shots and saw this little honey come running in," Carter says, rubbing his jaw. "What the hell is going on?"

"You see anyone else?" asks what seems to be the commanding officer.

Carter shrugs. "Just her."

The other cops fan out.

Jack and I crawl to the window and look down. There's

a sheer drop to the dock of maybe thirty feet below. I figure we can clear the dock and hit water with enough of a jump. Jack zips up his jacket and slowly inches the window open, cursing under his breath at the misaligned jambs groaning in protest. He pulls himself out the window as the flashlight beams ricochet around the warehouse.

"I'll jump first," he says. "Then you jump and I'll help you to the dock, okay?"

I nod. What a clusterfuck.

Jack lowers himself out the window and hangs from the ledge by his hands. He draws up his legs, presses his feet against the wall, and uncoils into a backflip over the dock and into the water feet first. Even in my terror I'm impressed.

I look down from the pallets one last time. Carter and Carmen are gone, but cops are everywhere. Some are looking up into the rafters and I duck back. Fuck. Into the water it is.

I'm pretty sure that I can clear the dock, but cleanly entering the water seems doubtful. I wonder if I should hazard a hands-first dive or just cannonball into the dark surf. No fucking way I could backflip. I ease backward out onto the ledge and push hard with my legs, arching back toward the water.

I had hoped to rotate my feet around my head, landing feet-first into the water, but halfway down I know it's hopeless. As the wind builds to a roar in my ears, I tuck myself into a ball and clamp my hands over my face. The wet slap of water pushes the air from my lungs as I plunge into the ocean, sinking deep into the black water. I claw for the surface, not really sure which way is up. I start to feel the icy fingers of panic at my throat just as Jack grabs me by the wrist. We break the surface and I gasp for air.

We reach the barnacled pier and push along the slimy wall looking for ladders. The flashing glare of cruiser lights limns everything red, blue, purple. The water sucks the warmth from my body and my fingers go numb within moments. By the time Jack finds a ladder on the side of the pier, I'm struggling to hold on to the barnacle-encrusted rungs. I hook my arm through one rung and rest, shivering and angry, and then follow Jack to the top.

We creep along the warehouse wall until we reach the chain-link fence at the docking entrance. I peer carefully across the mouth of the warehouse and see Carmen led out in handcuffs to a parked cruiser. The tears on her face gleam in the harsh dock lights. We watch the deputy secure her in the backseat and then trot back into the warehouse.

Standing there shivering and wet, a black rage builds in me. I curse myself for acquiescing to Carter.

Carmen has her face in her hands, shoulders shaking. "I'm going to grab that cruiser and get her," Jack says.

"You'll never make it." I touch his arm, but he shakes it off.

We watch in dismay as another cruiser rolls into the dockyard and parks. A female police officer steps out, holding the hand of the little girl.

Jack's shoulders slump. Another shiver goes through both of us. "Maybe they'll leave. I only need a minute to wire it and then we're gone."

"Jack, they're not going to leave," I say.

Jack hugs himself and paces back and forth. The female cop gets into the front of the cruiser and starts talking to Carmen.

"Jack, we have to go."

Jack closes his eyes and takes a breath. "Yeah, okay."

"We'll have to swim, before the copters show up. Come on."

To my relief he follows me back to the pier.

I jump into the cold black water. It's relatively calm and we try to stay underwater as much as we can, but by the end I'm exhausted and dog paddling, with Jack helping me along.

We pull ourselves out of the water just as the helicopters show up and the arriving lights of more police cruisers create a kaleidoscope rainbow against the water and warehouses.

July 12, 1986, 5:21 P.M.

"I don't care if she's the fucking tooth fairy."

The bell tinkles as the door to the Sweet Tooth opens. I'm expecting Victor, but instead Carter and some guy I've never seen before walk in. The other man is older than Carter, his black hair flecked with steel gray and the lines on his face pulled down by gravity. The old wooden floor creaks as they approach the counter.

"Mrs. Pagnolli?" the new guy asks Cora with a smile.

She sends back a delicate smile of her own. "Call me Cora."

He withdraws his badge from his coat and holds it out for her to see. "I'm a special agent for the Federal Bureau of Investigation, Cora. My name is Larry Holland. This is my partner, Carter Hansen."

Cora brushes some stray strands of hair from her face with a slightly trembling hand. "What do you want?"

"Cora, we have reason to believe that your husband's business interests are a cloak for felonies and fraud." He pauses to wait for her reaction.

"I don't know what you're talking about," I interject. "We make truffles here."

Larry ignores me and removes some pictures from his coat. He slides one across the counter to Cora. "Have you seen this man before, Cora?"

I slide over and we both peer at the photograph. I actually don't recognize him. Just another corpse. "No," Cora says. "But I'll tell my husband you stopped by. We have work to do. Please excuse us." She smiles politely at them and turns toward the kitchen.

"Excuse you? I don't think so," Larry says. He flings the picture at her as she retreats. "That man died in agony, and he died without saying good-bye to his son and daughter. He died because of your husband."

"You like picking on old women?" I snap at him.

"I don't care if she's the fucking tooth fairy," Larry says.

"Why don't you assholes take a walk?"

"No, wait here," Cora says and disappears into the back room.

"Let me say this loud and clear," Larry says to me. "Your boss is a bad guy."

Who the fuck is this asswipe? Who would want to partner with Carter? I put my hands on the counter. "Show me your warrant or arrest me. Anything else is harassment."

"Larry," Carter says, "maybe we—"

Cora walks back into the room with a photo album in her arms. I'm surprised to see her face red with anger.

"My Victor is so evil, yes?" Cora says. "You blame him for everything? I have some of my own pictures." She flings open the thick album and thrusts a finger at a photo. "See this little girl? Victor rescued her from Cambodia. And her? She and her sister were starving in Mexico City." She flips through several other pictures. "My husband saves these girls. He educates them, brings them to the United States. Gives them a job, a life. He doesn't have to do this. So tell me if Victor is as evil as you say, why does he save so many children?"

"Guilty conscience," Larry drawls.

Cora points to the door. "Get out!" she screeches and heaves the album at him, pictures flying from the book and fluttering to the floor.

"You tell your husband we'll be back," Larry says. He strolls out of the shop with Carter on his heels.

Cora puts her face in her hands and sobs. I give her an awkward hug, wondering who the hell Larry is and why would he suddenly care about us. Carter never mentioned him.

Victor arrives just moments later. He looks at Cora weeping and then the mess on the floor. "What's happened?"

"Just a friendly visit from Carter and his new buddy," I say.

"Buddy?"

"Yeah, looks like he has a partner now. Some old asshole named Larry."

Victor nods. "Carter still looking for his gun?"

"I guess it's still missing, which is lucky for me. But they were here for something else."

Cora excuses herself to the kitchen, and I bend down to pick up the loose pictures. Victor helps me, looking more mystified than angry. He picks up an old photo from the floor and shows it to me. "Recognize her?"

I see myself from thirteen years ago, facing the lens with a troubled frown. I remember Father Ramirez asking me to smile—"*Sonrisa para la cámara!*"—but I refused. Victor picks up another photo and shakes his head. It's a picture of a new girl who just came in, Maria Gonzales.

"We need to make a stop," Victor says. "Father Ramirez wants me to check on her. She hasn't come around in over a week. I'll talk to Carter later."

"We need Roland?" I ask.

"I don't think so," Victor says. "Maria probably just doesn't want to listen to his sermons. I don't blame her."

Forty minutes later we're cruising into downtown, the high rises blocking out the late afternoon sun and casting deep shadows into the alleys.

What Cora said is true. Victor does sponsor a lot of girls and young women. I was one of them. Not all the girls acclimate, however. It's not easy.

We arrive at Maria's address and slowly circle the block a few times. I don't like to be rushed. I could cut corners and make mistakes. Fall into bad habits that get people killed. But nothing looks out of the ordinary, so I park in the garage. Despite Victor's protests, we take the stairs up three flights.

By the time we reach the landing, Victor is panting. "You are so damn paranoid, Reno. Jesus." He leans against the doorjamb. "What's wrong with letting a fat man take the elevator once in a while?" He looks up at me and smiles, just like the old mischievous Victor who would laugh at himself.

I swing the fire door open. The hallway is empty. So far so good. I step lightly down the hallway, looking for the right apartment number. We stop at the door and Victor knocks softly. No answer.

"Think she's even home?" Victor asks.

I look down the long narrow hallway again. Nobody in sight. I press my ear against the door. Nothing. No television, no radio. I knock on the door, louder this time. Still nothing. I look at Victor with raised eyebrows.

"Father Ramirez said some guy named Mortado might be trying to pimp her," he says. "Get us in."

I check the hallway again. Probably a few eyeballs peer through the peepholes. I glance at Victor, whose face is set with determination. He always gets this way when one of his wayward girls is in trouble. Screw it. I press into the cheap door, flexing the frame. A quick knee into the knob and the door pops open.

I walk into the living room. Sprawled on the couch, clothed only in panties and a T-shirt, is a teenage girl. Maria, no doubt. She appears to be asleep, a gossamer thread of drool stretching from one lip to the carpeted floor. I scan the kitchen, then sweep the bedroom. I duck my head in the small bathroom off the bedroom and return, confident that we're alone.

Victor picks up a syringe from the window sill and holds it up. The needle's tip glitters in the sun. "This breaks my heart. Who would do this to her? Help me get her up, will you?"

I grab Maria by the shoulders and sit her up on the couch. Her head lolls and she opens her eyes. She gives me a bleary look and a goofy smile. "*Hola…*" she slurs.

Victor picks up a pair of dirty blue sweatpants off the floor. "Help me get her dressed."

Maria protests sleepily as we push her arms and legs into the sweats, but I'm issuing a stream of Spanish at her, arguing and prodding. The girl finally nods, giving us another wide smile.

"Let's get out of here," Victor says.

I squat, put my shoulder at Maria's hip and press up, slinging her over my shoulder in a fireman's carry. I estimate she probably only weighs 90 pounds. I move slowly toward the door, trying to find an angle so I don't clip her head against the frame. Just as I reach the door, it suddenly swings open and hits Maria on her skeletal hip.

"*Mierda!*" I cry and stagger back, trying to not drop her.

A bull of a man in blazing blue sweats pushes against the door, seemingly confused that it didn't open fully. I retreat into the living room.

Mortado, I bet. Just my luck.

"*¡Qué chingados… ?!*" he says. A giant frown pinches his face.

"We're friends of Maria," I say.

"You don't look like friends to me," Mortado says.

I dip to one knee, duck my head, and let Maria roll from my shoulder onto the floor. She moans and curls into a ball.

Mortado kicks the apartment door shut behind him. "You stealing my property? You gotta pay for her if you want her."

I try to keep my voice reasonable. "Do you know who he is?" I ask, tilting my head toward Victor.

"You bust into my crib and steal my bitch, I don't care who you are."

"Are you the one who gave her the drugs?" asks Victor. He holds up the syringe.

"She owes me," Mortado says. "Bitch did more than she could afford. Maybe if you got the cash to pay for it, I'll let you walk."

Victor's face hardens.

"Hey, you ain't got the cash, it's cool." Mortado nods at me. "I'll take this one. You take Maria, we call it even." He takes a couple large strides across the room and reaches for me.

I step back into the kitchen and push his arm so he half-spins around. "I don't think so," I sneer, waiting for him to plant his leg to counter the swing. When he does, I kick his braced knee and he falls heavily onto a filthy rug on the linoleum. After a flash of surprise and pain, his faces darkens and he pulls a butterfly knife from his jacket. He jumps at me, twirling the knife, the blade flinging open between the metal clasps that quickly become the shaft. A memory flickers of another knife, just like this one. He closes the distance before I can pull my Glock.

I find my balance, take a half-step, and lash out my foot, kicking his knife arm at the elbow. I had hoped to break it, but I don't hear the snap of bone, just his roar of pain. Worse yet, he doesn't drop the knife.

Switching the knife to his left hand, he feints left and then charges, knife held high.

I dodge the blade, but he uses his body to barge me into the wall with a heavy thud. The drywall cracks as I gasp with surprise and pain. I had been too intent on the knife, and he moved more quickly than I expected. I try to squirm free, but he pins me with one arm and brings his knife up and then sharply in, looking to skewer me. I twist and the knife slashes across my abdomen.

His arm comes up and back in again. I brace against the wall and press into him. I feel the blade slice across my back and gouge into the drywall. He's way too heavy for me to push off, and I regret not bringing Roland. I should have just shot him when he walked in.

Out of the corner of my eye, I see Victor take two strides and slam the syringe into Mortado's ear, who lets out an agonized, infuriated shriek. Face crumpled with shock and pain, Mortado pulls the syringe from his ear with a roar.

He flings it against the wall and brings up his knife to spear Victor.

Victor jumps back, but trips over Maria's unconscious body. As he's scrambling back, I punt Mortado between the legs.

He falls forward, screeching in a high wail. He collapses into twisted ball on the floor next to Maria. My foot flashes out and catches his chin from the side and Mortado's piercing scream abruptly stops. Air continues to roar out of his nose. His jaw is clearly broken. Teeth jut through his smashed lips, forming an inane, lopsided smile.

Victor climbs to his feet and we look at each other, both breathing heavily.

I grimace, touching the long but shallow slash above my bellybutton. Damn it. More scars. "That asshole almost got me. Jesus."

Victor puffs his cheeks and blows out a jet of air. He smiles at me. "Just like the old days."

July 18, 1986, 9:13 P.M.

"Hike the skirt."

I drift through traffic, easing the sedan into gaps as they appear. A headache pounds in my temple. Roland slouches in the passenger seat, his right leg bouncing with tension. He lights a cigarette and cracks the window.

"Uh, uh. Not in the car."

"Come on, Reno. Shit, just one. Ease up."

I whip my right hand out and flick the cigarette from Roland's lips and out the window. The car jerks halfway out of our lane, but it's worth it.

Roland rubs his face. "I'll just light another one."

"And I'll knock that one away too."

"No, you won't."

"Try me," I say. "Those things will kill you anyway."

"Lung cancer at least has the decency to wait until I'm old. By that time Angie and the baby can take care of themselves." He wipes his face again. "I need some nicotine. I couldn't sleep last night."

"Me, either. Why you?"

Roland grimaces. "I got a lot of saliva."

I squint at him. "What?"

"Saliva. I got to spit it out."

"Just swallow it."

Roland shakes his head. "No way. I don't swallow spit."

"Everyone does."

"You want to swallow my spit?" Roland asks.

I wave my hand at him. "You're missing the whole damn point. Everyone swallows their own spit. It's unavoidable."

"All I'm saying is—"

The privacy glass slides down. "You're weaving," Victor grumbles.

"I'm helping Roland quit smoking."

"You look nice tonight, Reno," Victor says. "The old man will appreciate the gesture."

I feel myself blush, which infuriates me. I'd give anything to control my blushing. "I'm still worried. Let me go in first, check it out."

Victor snorts. "Yeah, I'm sure Gartello will give you a personal tour. You need to relax. If you're so worried, call Salvatore."

"I did. No answer."

Victor shrugs. "It'll be fine. Worst case I'll apologize, and we'll have to even it out with the Russian pricks." He sits back and raises the privacy glass again.

I knew Gartello appreciated a little formality in a world that, so far as he was concerned, had gone to shit. So I had worn my best skirt. My only skirt. And honest-to-God pantyhose. Last time I had done that had been, well, the last dinner with Gartello. What little cleavage I have is pushed up to the top of my silk blouse.

Roland's leg twitches in a continual nervous beat. I shoot him a look. "What's going on? You cool?"

He shrugs. "Yeah, no worries. Why?"

I look at him more closely. "You jumpin' tonight?"

He pauses for a moment, then nods guiltily.

"You can't be flying on the job," I snap. "I can't have you cranked. You have to be steady."

"Hey, it's not like I planned it, okay? You call out of the blue, told me you were swinging by. What did you want me to do?"

"Just tell me next time, don't make me guess on my own."

"Yeah, yeah, okay," he mutters.

"It's not like I had a choice. If Gartello tells us to come over, we come over."

"He pissed?"

"What do you think?" I'm pretty damn sure our botched warehouse job wasn't going to please Gartello. Victor didn't seem concerned but I'm worried.

I pull into Gartello's drive and the guard at the gate waves us through.

Crickets chorus in the warm summer night. A couple of bodyguards on the entrance pat down Roland and Victor. They find Roland's pistol. "I can keep it, or you can put it in the car," the guy says.

"Keep it," Roland says.

"I'm clean," I say, holding up my hands.

A guy I've never seen before shakes his head. "Everyone is patted. You know the rules." He gives me a small smile.

New rules. But finally some sort of security for Gartello. I take a step back. "And just where do you think I'm hiding a gun?" The skirt and the blouse don't conceal much. I spin around, giving them a full look.

Victor and Roland stand in the doorway, waiting. "Come

on, Reno, don't make trouble," Roland says. "Just let him do his job."

"Hike the skirt," the bigger one grunts, unconvinced.

I stare at them for a moment and then sneer. "Screw off."

"Reno…" Victor says.

I pull up my dress and jut out my hip. I let them stare at my black silk panties, swivel, and give them a good look at my ass. "Happy now?"

The smaller of the two raises his eyebrows. He gestures to his partner and they part, letting me pass.

"Assholes," I say as I walk into Gartello's mansion. I'm happy for the new men and higher security, but that was ridiculous. Still no sign of Salvatore. I'll give him hell as soon as I see him.

Roland leads us down the familiar hallway. I admire the carpet, the intricate designs and interwoven colors reminding me of my childhood in Colombia. Gartello's gruff manner also reminds me of home, of the *llaneros* who worked the ranches with dignity and grace.

Another man opens the door at the end of the hallway, providing us entry into Gartello's study. I've never seen him before either—maybe Salvatore finally got some smarter guys. I walk into the room, wanting to rip Salvatore a new one, but he isn't there.

A handful of men fill the room. A small table away from Gartello's old wooden desk has been set up for dinner. There's no sign of Gartello. I don't recognize anyone. They loiter, not meeting my gaze and suddenly nothing feels right to me. When the door closes behind us, I hear the quick *snick* of the deadbolt. I flash a look at Roland. He heard it too. He looks nonchalant, but I see his eyes darting around the room.

He's almost vibrating from the speed coursing through his bloodstream and the sudden tension.

I swallow and move slightly in front of Victor as a door across the room opens. Anatoli Zhukov walks in with Golnak at his side. Zhukov's titanium white hair flashes in the bright sconce lighting.

Golnak gives me a black stare.

Adrenaline floods me, and I start to perspire. I take a long quiet breath and wonder if there is another exit from the room. I count the men. Nine, not counting Zhukov. Three of them stand in front of the window. No way out there.

Zhukov grins at Victor, his smile like a suture around his teeth. "Pleasing to see you again, Victor."

"Where's Gartello?"

Zhukov tries to look hurt. "Poor man is detained. Very sad."

No doubt Gartello has been detained in plastic bags in Zhukov's car trunk. A wave of deep sadness fills me, but I push it aside and bring my full attention back to the other men in the room. Their jackets don't hang right, and I'm sure guns are slung under their armpits.

Zhukov gestures at a nearby table. "I prepare late dinner. I bring champagne and truffle. But no caviar. You forgive me, yes? I am all out." He raises his hands to the ceiling and then lets them flop down to his sides. "I hope maybe you bring caviar with you."

Victor just looks at him, his face stony. I know the look. He is murderously mad now. He might not have seen the guns or heard the door lock or even recognized the killing zone he stood in, but he's realized his friend and mentor Gartello is gone.

"This isn't about caviar," Victor says quietly.

"True," Zhukov says, his hands folded into a steeple. "This is about the weak and the strong."

"You killed him," Victor says flatly.

Zhukov rubs his jaw and his dead eyes linger on me for a moment. "When I was child, my father remind me to always know thickness of ice because if you fall through, you cannot climb back."

Victor looks around the room. "You think it will all end here? It won't."

Zhukov smiles. "Here begins for me. But for you, yes, I think ice is too thin."

I turn my head a fraction, trying to catch Roland's eye. His pale face is focused on Zhukov. Just then the phone on the desk next to Zhukov rings. Before anyone else reacts, Roland darts forward, picks it up, and puts it to his ear. "Yeah? Who? Oh, yeah, he's right here. Hang on."

Roland shakes the phone. "Mr. Zhukov, sir, it's for you. It's Gartello. He says he wants a word with you."

The whole room freezes. Zhukov squints at Roland and then sends a questioning glance at Golnak, who looks just as baffled.

Roland extends the phone to Zhukov, then hands it to Golnak when the Russian puts out his hand to stop Roland from getting too close. As Golnak brings the receiver to his ear, Roland jerks Golnak's other arm sharply forward and pivots behind him, snatching what looks like a mini-Uzi from Golnak's shoulder holster.

I yank Victor to the floor.

Golnak slams Roland against the wall. Roland staggers but manages to spray the room with bullets. Golnak twists away from Roland and pushes a startled Zhukov under the dinner table. Splinters of wood and broken glass fill the room. A man screams. Golnak tips over the dinner table, sending the plates tumbling to the floor, and scrambles over it for cover.

I roll back toward the locked door and kick a man hard in the knee. He falls heavily to the carpet as a burst from Roland's stolen Uzi mutes the injured man's screams.

I reach around the fallen man's shoulder and jerk his Uzi from his holster. His fist comes toward my face, but I duck and catch it on the top of my head. I nearly faint from the blow but pull the trigger just as the muzzle clears his holster. His body jerks and he makes a wet gurgle as his throat is ripped away by the stream of bullets.

I survey the room. It's chaos. Many of Zhukov's men are down. The survivors seek cover and try to avoid catching each other with their crossfire. Roland has no such compunctions. He roars through a full clip, spaying the room again. Broken glass and shredded upholstery fill the air. I smell cordite and blood.

Golnak huddles behind the dinner table. He raises a pistol and pumps several shots toward Roland. Roland returns fire and Golnak ducks.

I pull Victor onto his feet. The door to the room starts to open, and I kick it hard, putting all of my fear and energy into the kick. It swings practically off its hinges, right into the face of another guard. He holds a gun but is momentarily stunned by the door's impact. I catch him above the sternum with a burst from my Uzi and Victor and I sprint down the hallway. I stoop and retrieve the fallen man's gun as I run by. At the door I shove Victor behind me and roll onto the porch, holding down the trigger. A man kneeling on the side of the doorframe doubles over as I strafe him with my gun. I grab Victor again and pull him to the car. From behind I hear screaming and shouts in Russian, punctuated by the chatter of the Uzis.

I push Victor into the back of the sedan. As I run around the rear of the car, I smash both lights with the Uzi. I reach the driver's seat in a few more strides. Turning the keys in the ignition, I ram the gear into reverse. The engine roars as I stomp the accelerator and spin the wheels onto the porch near the front door, cracking the stairs and one post. Flashes of gunfire from within the house cast a series of staccato shadows on the doorway. Another man runs around the corner of the house. I stick my arm out the window and drop him with the last burst from the Uzi.

"Let's go, let's go!" roars Victor.

"No, Roland's not out yet!"

"Throw me a gun!"

"Just keep down!" I bark. I throw the empty Uzi under the seat, open the glove box, grab my Glock, and lean out the window. Anyone but Roland coming through the door gets a double tap.

I pray for Roland. *Hurry, hurry,* I urge him, and then he staggers onto the porch, a huge blossom of blood staining his shirt. I jerk the transmission into park and scramble from the sedan just as he falls heavily to the ground. I reach him just as another man, also covered in blood and staggering, appears in the doorway. I fire directly into his chest and he falls back into the darkness beyond the door. I hook Roland under his armpits and drag him toward the sedan. He is slick with blood and everything begins to move slowly for me.

Another man runs from the doorway. I drop Roland and he tumbles to the ground with a pathetic murmur of pain. I desperately bring up my gun just as the man pulls the trigger. His muzzle flash blinds me and I feel a hot burn on my ear. I have the sensation of floating as my gun bucks twice in my hand. The man falls to the ground writhing and screaming. I turn and find Roland pawing at the car door. He's still alive, and I can breathe again.

Victor jerks open the door and awkwardly pulls Roland into the sedan. They fall into the backseat together and I kick the door shut. My ears buzz like angry bees, injured by the gunfire. Another man's shocked white face, his lips almost invisible, materializes from the side of the car and my gun kicks in a two-step cadence. He falls before me. I slide across the still-warm hood of the car and turtle into the driver's seat.

I clunk the transmission into drive and gun it. The big sedan's wheels spin in place for a moment and then we lunge forward. My headlights blind two men with hands fisted around pistols in the driveway. Their strained faces briefly flash in the light before the car pulls them under. I fishtail slightly, then shoot down the driveway.

Distantly I can hear Roland gasping in pain. Victor squirms in the seat, cursing, as I jerk the car onto the highway. I mash the accelerator to the floor. The tachometer jumps, and the car rushes down the road.

Beams of pursuing headlights swing behind us and rim Victor with a halo of light. Are they gaining? It's hard to tell in the dark. I weave through the late-night traffic, trying to steady myself. Built for power and security, the sedan's top speed isn't as high as I need and our pursuers are catching up, their lights brightening as they near.

I switch off my headlights. The road becomes a dark strip, the bits of glass and pebbles in the road reflecting like stars in the night sky. I hope that my broken taillights coupled with no headlights will make me practically invisible in the darkness. I grit my teeth and focus on the road, waiting for the last second to swing hard onto the fork toward town.

Muzzle flashes appear in the rearview mirror. Pressing hard for the city limits, I pass another car at 120 mph. I still feel the wooden shock of the fight numbing my mind.

Guided by only the streetlights, I plunge through an intersection and then aim for a narrow alley on my left. I brake too late and overshoot it, pulverizing a mailbox as I skid onto the sidewalk. The bang of the exploding mailbox snaps me out of my floaty shock. I fumble for my seatbelt and yell at Victor to do the same. "Belt up! Try to hook up Roland!"

I slide into the next alley and surge down the darkness, barely discerning the telephone poles and dumpsters as we flash by. I twist through another alley and barrel down a one-way street. Soon only one car remains behind us, its lights no doubt picking up the reflective paint on my license plate. It has to be that asshole Golnak. A surge of anger floods me.

I sweep onto Hammett Street and slow to let the pursuing car catch up. The chatter of submachine gun fire and the hard thumps against the body panel signal their arrival. My side window suddenly webs from the impact of bullets and goes opaque. I breathe a prayer of thanks for the Lexan.

A man leans out, aiming his gun low at my tires. "What are you doing?" Victor shouts right before I jerk the wheel, slam into the other vehicle, and crush the man between the cars. He screams, his gun spasmodically shooting into the asphalt. His bones splinter wetly as he slides out of the window and pinwheels onto the blacktop. Fuck him. Fuck all of them.

I catch a glimpse of Golnak in the driver's seat and sideswipe him again. The weight of my big sedan forces the lighter car to the side. Holding the wheel, I push Golnak's car over the curb, narrowly missing a power pole and then directly into an apartment building. His car smashes into the side, and I slide along the apartment wall, fighting to keep the bumper from catching, then clear it and flash through an intersection.

I floor it again and weave through alleys and side roads, the car just a streak of black in the darkness, barely missing a pair of garbage men slinging trash into their truck. I hear a wailing siren and turn away from it.

I crane my head around and see Roland slack in the backseat covered in his blood. His eyes flutter at me.

"He needs a doctor," I say to Victor. "We have to get to an ER."

Roland groans and tries to sit up. "No ER. No cops."

Victor shakes his head. "Roland, you need help."

"No cops..."

He fumbles at a key hanging from a metal chain around his neck. He tries to pull it off but lacks the strength. "Make sure Angie gets this, okay?"

"Sure, Roland, but we're gonna take care of you. You're gonna be fine."

"No cops. Promise me. I can't go back."

"Don't worry, Roland."

"Promise..." He falls back in the seat, silent.

I slow down, confident that we've evaded or killed all of Zhukov's men. I suddenly realize that we're near the hospital I visited weeks ago. Gathering my bearings, I recognize the cross street and moments later squeal into the ER parking lot. The big red cross mounted above the doors tinges the night with crimson light.

I park and begin wiggling out of my pantyhose.

"What the hell are you doing now?" Victor asks.

"I'm taking care of Roland, that's what I'm doing." I rip a leg from my pantyhose and slide the loose end over my head.

"Reno," Victor begins, his voice low and dangerous. "Start the car. You're not doing this. I'm not losing both of you."

I grab my Glock. "I'll be right back."

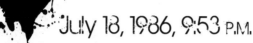# July 18, 1986, 9:53 P.M.

"One day your sister will end up dead on your front lawn."

I open the car door before Victor can reply and sprint barefoot across the parking lot and into the waiting room. Startled patients and a nurse shrink back, looks of horror and fear twisting their faces. I brandish my pistol and brush past them and into the examination area. More nurses turn around. One drops a clipboard and ducks behind her desk. Another flees down an adjoining hallway. I ignore them. Where the fuck are all the doctors?

I swiftly go from room to room, opening and closing doors. The first room is empty, the second occupied by a lone patient. The third room, however, yields my prize. A man in green scrubs and blue jeans stands listening with a black stethoscope to the chest of an elderly man. I put the Glock to his head. "Doc, you need to come with me. Right now."

He turns his head and sees the gun. "Don't shoot," he yelps.

I grunt in surprise. It's Dr. Barrington. "Sorry, Doc, but I need your help." I grab his arm and yank him from the room. I pull him down the hallway toward the exit, eager to get out before I run into any organized resistance.

I catch sight of a faceless woman coming toward me, wearing what seems to be a bloody, ripped shroud. She looks like an apparition from the crypt. It takes an instant before I recognize myself in the mirror's reflection at the end of the hall. No wonder people just stared in horror when I burst in. *Dios mío.*

"Don't get in the way. Let her through," Barrington is yelling to the nurses. "Don't shoot them," he says to me. "They won't hurt you."

"We need a surgical kit, something for gunshots. Where do you keep that stuff?"

He motions to a nearby room and I drag him over, kicking open the door. "Get all the stuff you're gonna need for a surgery. Gunshot to the abdomen."

He stops, sucks in some air. "We'll need blood. We don't have it right here."

"Grab what you can. We don't have any more time."

"At least let me get some ex-lap trays." Shaking his head and muttering, he grabs what look like sterile blue paper pouches. I take one package in my loose hand while he cradles the rest in his arms. He wants more, but I pull him out and hope it is enough.

I see Victor's face pressed up against the sedan's window. I motion to him and he pushes open the driver's side door. I shove Barrington across the front seat, past the steering wheel. "Get in, Doc, we're going for a ride."

He slides over without comment, and I follow closely behind. "Keep sliding, Doc. All the way over, that's it." I hand my Glock to Victor, who puts it to Barrington's head.

Two seconds later, I pull sharply out of the lot and

accelerate up the street. "Okay, I got a doctor," I say to Victor. "Where to?"

"Yeah, I see that," Victor snaps. "Take the next left. Best bet right now is Benny's."

"*Benny's?*"

"You got a better idea?"

At least it was close by. Benjamin Wah, a veterinarian, provides favors to Victor occasionally, mostly fencing various drugs though his labs. I glance over at Roland. "How's he doing?"

"Drifting in and out."

I grab Barrington's scrubs and yank him toward the gap between the front seats. "Keep him alive."

Barrington simply climbs over the seat and sidles over to Roland. He feels around Roland's throat, lifts his eyelids, and shines a light. "Ragged pulse. He needs a hospital."

"Not going to happen," Victor says quickly. "You're all he's got."

I pull into the parking lot of Benny's Animal Hospital and park behind the building. Victor kicks open the back door and I jump out to help Barrington carry a moaning Roland into the surgery bay and slide him onto a cold stainless steel table.

Barrington looks around in horror. "You've got to be kidding me. You expect me to operate here?"

Victor glowers at Barrington and points my Glock at him. "Get to work or I'll shoot you dead right here. You understand me?"

Barrington flinches but then simply says, "Okay, let's go."

I flick on all the lights and Barrington begins to scrub

up in the sink, pouring copious amounts of brown prep soap on his hands. He points at Victor. "If he gains consciousness, you'll have to restrain him." He nods at me. "I'm going to need your help. Lose the skirt and blouse. They're filthy."

I unzip the skirt and slip out of my blouse. In just my bra and panties, I shoulder next to Barrington and vigorously scrub my hands and arms.

"Face too," grunts Barrington, all business now as he rolls open the surgical kits. "You've got blood all over you."

I rip off the nylon stocking, blow the hair from my eyes, run soap around my neck and face, and then dip my entire head under the faucet. By the time I towel off, Barrington is irritably waving me over. "Reno!" he says in surprise. "I didn't recognize you."

"Sorry, Doc, I didn't plan this. You were just in the wrong place at the wrong time."

He hands me a pair of thin latex gloves. He examines Roland and says tersely, "Okay, looks like five entry wounds. Help me turn him onto his back. I need to see how many exited and where."

As we roll Roland over, he groans and opens his eyes. For a brief moment his eyes focus on me. "Reno... just like my dream..." he slurs. "The lights... I can hear the music..."

I caress his head. "Just take it easy, Roland. We're taking care of you." He closes his eyes and says nothing.

"Two exit wounds, anterior," Barrington mutters to himself. "Small caliber, probably thirty-eight or nine-millimeter." He squints at me as he quickly hooks up an IV and stabs a thick needle into Roland. "He'll get a liter of fluid as far as it will go in and as much morphine as he can handle." He hands me what looks like two big silver serving spoons.

"Retract with these." He sees my confusion and says, "We're going to find those three missing bullets and see if there's any fecal spillage. I need you to hold him open so I can move around."

Roland is slack now, deep into the morphine.

I nod, but nausea grips me when Barrington draws a scalpel from Roland's sternum to navel. Another quick slice across his belly opens a big flap of skin. Barrington cuts through what looks like muscle, and I see Roland's intestines protrude. Ragged holes perforate muscle and skin.

Barrington curses. "Damn it. One of his kidneys got hit." He glances at me. "You okay?"

I manage a nod.

"I'm going to ligate his renal veins and arteries," he says after a moment. "You'll need to clamp that big vessel shut when I do. See it?" He points with his scalpel at what looked to me like a thick pulsing red worm.

I nod as sweat pours down my face.

"I won't be able to save it," Barrington says. "Not here. He can get by with just one kidney. Ready?"

I turn my head and vomit. It splashes on the floor. The copper tang of blood mixes with the sweet rot of puke and I heave again.

"Reno!" Barrington barks me. "Get it together or your friend is going to die."

I nod again and start to wipe my mouth. "No! Don't let your hands touch it. I need them as sterile as possible. Now, on my count. On three, clamp it off and I'll stitch it closed. One, two, three!"

He makes two slices on either end of the dark red kidney,

pulls the entire organ from the cavity, and tosses it on the floor. It splatters into my vomit.

I grip the artery, my hand shaking.

"Tighter!" barks Barrington.

I squeeze as hard as I can manage while Barrington squints and jabs his needle along the end, tying it off. He finishes quickly, then draws stitches through two more nicked arteries that were sluggishly spurting blood.

He grunts. "Not good. He's got no blood pressure. Shit, we're losing him. There's got to be another big leak." He digs through Roland's intestines, blue ropes covered in blood, and pushes them to the side, gesturing for me to hold them. I dig my hands into Roland's guts and begin to cry. I turn my head, but a few tears drop into Roland anyway.

Barrington's face clenches into a tight fist of anger. "Son of a bitch. He's chewed up. He barely has a pulse." He whips another strand of suture through a needle and spends several minutes rapidly pulling the thread in and out of Roland's wounds.

Roland begins to shake. His body flops on the table for several seconds. "Hold him steady!" Barrington barks at Victor. I watch him feverishly sew, whipping the suture in and out Roland's wounds. I think Roland's breathing feels too shallow and I close my eyes, praying that he won't die. When I open my eyes again, Barrington is breathing heavily with his head low against the table.

"Why are you stopping?"

"He's gone, Reno. I'm sorry."

"What? What do you mean? He's dead?"

He raises his head. "See this?" He points to a reddish-brown rubbery looking thing. "That's his liver. It took a slug in the dome. I'm surprised he made it this far." He stands back from the table and strips off his gloves.

Tears run down my face. I should have just told Victor to go to hell and brought Roland into the ER. I could have saved him… I sob once, my hand covering my mouth. Goddammit. Goddamn Zhukov. Goddamn Carter and his caviar. Goddamn everything.

"I did everything I could for him. He was just too far gone."

I lean down and gently kiss Roland's ashen forehead. I hold my breath, trying to keep it all inside. I clamp my hand over my mouth but the sobs rip through.

After a minute, I walk over and kneel next to Victor, who is sprawled on the floor against the wall. He's still holding my Glock. "Roland didn't make it."

Victor presses the heels of his hand to his eyes. "I know." We sit in silence for a few moments. Victor sighs. "The fucking Russians. I should have seen it coming."

He stands up and gently draws me to my feet. "Roland wouldn't want you to cry, kiddo. He knew the rules." We stand there in silence and he hands me the pistol. "What do you want to do with the doctor?"

I wipe the tears from my cheeks and sniff, looking over at Barrington, who's leaning against the wall with his eyes closed. "I was thinking he could probably help us, you know? Never have enough doctors…"

Victor scowls. "He can't be much of a doctor. Couldn't do anything for Roland. Just take care of him."

"Look, he'll keep this quiet," I say. "Just give me a moment, okay?"

Victor sighs and waves his hand dismissively. "Make

sure he knows what he's getting into. Explain it to him very clearly."

I walk back to Barrington, who watches me with frightened eyes.

"Give me your wallet, Doc."

"W-why?" he stammers.

"Just do it, okay?" I hold out my hand and stare at him until he complies.

I flip the wallet open and hold up a finger before he can protest. "Under no circumstances do you talk to him," I say, tilting my head toward Victor. "Just stay here and be quiet."

I stride down the hallway and dial Carter on the desk phone. "It's Reno."

"What's up, Reno?" Carter answers sleepily. "You horny?"

"Never going to happen," I reply. I hold up Barrington's driver's license to the light. "I need next of kin and current addresses for Franklin Barrington. B-a-r-r-i-n-g-t-o-n, 384 East Townsend."

"Right now?" complains Carter. "Let me talk to Victor. Look, I really have to get my gun back. I know one of you has it."

"You don't want to talk to him right now, trust me. And I don't have your gun. It's probably in an evidence room somewhere. Use your weasel skills to find it."

"Reno—"

"Call me back." I give him the phone number, hang up, and walk back to Barrington.

He's winding down, the adrenaline bleeding away. "I probably could have saved him at the hospital," he grunts. He gestures at the surgery bay. Pictures of dogs hang on the walls. "I can't do anything here." His voice is a mix of weary regret and fear.

I take a breath. "Look, I'm sorry about being so rough in the ER. I didn't plan this. You okay?"

Barrington stares at his shoes. "Yeah."

The phone rings down the hall. I walk back and pick up the receiver. "Hey, this guy's a doctor," Carter says. "Is he involved in transplants? Does he got any livers?"

"Just give me his next of kin."

He gives me Barrington's information, then says, "He could really help me. The organ list is way too long and—"

I crash the receiver back onto the phone and return to the surgery bay. "Doc, look at me. This is important. Doc?" I draw his face up until his eyes meet mine. I can see that he's terrified. I feel badly for him. He's just a sweet kid.

"Doc? That's my boss. He needs to be convinced that you won't reveal our identities or other certain details about tonight."

"Oh, I'm not going to tell anyone about this. I won't say a word." He says it breathlessly, without any hesitation. "Tell him I won't say anything. It's cool."

I shake my head. "Doc, it's not cool. The cops are going to talk to you. A woman covered in blood dragged you out of an ER. They will want a story. They are going to push you."

I can see hope begin to light him up. "Don't worry about it. I'll just tell them I don't remember anything. I'll make something up."

Instead of responding, I just open his wallet and slide out two pictures. I know from Carter that they have to be his parents and sister. I hold them up to the light. "I know where your parents live. And your sister and her two kids."

Barrington looks puzzled. "What? What are you talking about?"

I press my lips together. I don't want to do this, but it's for his own sake, as well as mine. "Doc, if the cops come after us for this, my boss will kill your family. He'll hunt them down one at a time. He'll wait to kill you until the very last." I pause, watching the doctor's face twist with realization. "Don't let the Feds fool you, Frank. They won't be able to hide your entire family. One day your sister will end up dead on your front lawn." I pause to let it sink in. He stares at me raptly, his lips slightly open. "Frank, I know some really bad people. Do you understand?"

"Yes," he whispers.

"There's more," I continue evenly. "We might call you later. Ask you for a favor. Same rules apply."

Barrington swallows. He nods and reaches out for the photographs.

I pull them out of his reach. "Sorry, Doc. I think I'm going to keep these." I toss his wallet to him. "Now let's practice your story. Then you're going to tell it to my boss and convince him not to kill you right now. You ready?"

Barrington swallows. He looks at the pictures in my hand and licks his lips. "Yeah, okay," he croaks. "Whatever you say."

After twenty minutes of rehearsing his story, I pronounce him ready for Victor. As Barrington glumly stands at the stainless steel sink and washes up, I walk over to Victor.

"He's not going to cause any problems," I say.

Victor gives me a weary shrug. "You have good instincts, Reno. I should have listened to you earlier." He takes a breath and gets back to business. "I called Oscar. His crew will be here soon for the car and Roland. Do you want to stay with me tonight? Your apartment might not be safe."

"I'll be safe with Oscar. I need to take care of Roland."

"You sure about him?"

"Yeah."

"I won't question your instincts again."

"*You* sure?"

He grunts. "Absolutely."

Ten minutes later I hear the air brakes of what has to be Oscar's transport truck. I open the door after a quiet knock. Oscar slips in and takes a look at the operating bay. "*Que cagada!*" he says, averting his face.

Suddenly aware of being clad in just my bra and panties, I grab my dress lying on the floor but then drop it when I realize that it's just a bloody rag. "*Si, estoy de acuerdo,*" I say. "*Que es una mierda. Roland está muerto.*"

Oscar and his crew quickly enter the operating bay. Some of the men ogle me as they clean up. Oscar yells at them but quickly realizes it's useless. He strips off his shirt and hands it to me. I slide it over my head. It's still warm from his body. Oscar eyes his men and finally walks over to one about my height. They argue briefly in whispers and some of the men begin to laugh. To my surprise, the man abruptly quits arguing and slips off his jeans. Oscar ruffles his hair with a grin and then tosses the jeans along with the belt over to me. I gratefully pull them on. The men hoot as I cinch the belt.

They return to their work, gathering everything that's loose or covered in blood. Soon only Roland remains on the steel table. I hold his hand, fighting back the grief that will overwhelm me if I let it.

Oscar comes up to me looks at Roland. "He was your friend, but you know we must be quick…"

I nod, tears flooding my vision again.

Oscar nods at his men. They grab Roland and lug him out while I escort Barrington to the truck and watch two men wheel my sedan into the truck. Perforations from the automatic gunfire stitch the entire driver's side.

A flat piece of chain-link fence rests on the roof of the sedan. They sling Roland's limp body onto it as I help Victor into the back of the truck. Oscar gives us all one last look, and rolls down the door with a clatter. I hear him slam home the latch.

The truck starts and lurches backward as Oscar maneuvers onto the street and then trundles away. Before my eyes can adjust, the men in the back flick on flashlights. They wrap the chain link around Roland, cocooning him in mesh. They loop the ends with chain and pull the ends closed. I help crimp metal snap rings to the chain links. I've been through this routine before.

About twenty minutes later I feel the truck slow, the brakes easing out a low moan. The men ready themselves, each taking a hand on the mesh around Roland's body as they stare intently at the door. Victor sits moodily in the corner.

Moments later I hear the door latch ratchet back and the door rolls up, and a cool salt breeze swirls in. The men slide Roland off the roof and onto their shoulders.

"Wait!" I shout. I make the sign of the cross over Roland and pinch my fingers through the mesh and yank the tiny key dangling from the chain around his neck. The men shuffle back and forth, balancing Roland's body. I hurriedly find his left hand and twist off his wedding ring.

"Reno," Victor says softly. "We must be quick."

"Go," I say.

They walk to the edge of the truck, pausing for Oscar's signal. I hear the clanking of a buoy and realize where we are. Oscar has pulled over on a bridge over deep water, probably near the shipping channel.

Oscar pokes his head into the back of the truck. "Now!"

The men jump from the truck, Roland's body jostling around on their shoulders. They stagger to the side of the bridge and heave his corpse into the darkness. I hear the distant splash. They spring back into the truck, and Oscar rolls down the door.

I can smell the nervous sweat of the crew mixed with blood and gasoline. The beams of their flashlights dart around the space with each lurch of the truck. A heavy sadness grips me. I sob and shake. Roland deserved more.

Embarrassed or just wanting to give me privacy, the men turn off their flashlights and squat silently in the darkness as the truck bumps and squeaks along the highway.

July 18, 1986, 11:27 P.M.

"Just get through this night."

When we stop again, we're outside Victor's compound. I pull most of the men from the truck and direct them to sweep the grounds.

"You sure you don't want to stay here?" Victor asks.

"I'll be fine," I say. "Besides, I need to strip the weapons and the car."

"Oscar's men can do all that."

"No, they're staying here with you."

He shakes his head. "Reno…"

"I'll be fine."

Cora's standing in the doorway, her arms folded against the cold as she peers out in the darkness. Victor gives me a hard hug and reluctantly trudges across to Cora. He hugs her too and then closes the door.

I establish a perimeter with Oscar's men. Many of the younger ones look scared, but they're better than nothing. I grab Oscar to help me with the sedan.

By the time we pull into the junkyard, my sadness has hardened into anger. I help Oscar roll the sedan into the stripping stalls and soon the whirring of pneumatic tools fills the air as a group of men strip parts from the car. I have seen this before, but it still amazes me. Within twenty minutes only a husk of the car remains. Any object covered in blood is dipped in the muriatic acid Oscar uses for paint prepping. They pack the incinerator with everything inflammable. Seats, headliner, and carpet disappear into the maw. Then the crew throw their clothes into the glowing fire and march over to the yard hose for a vigorous spray from Oscar, who then throws them shop uniforms spattered with paint and grime.

After a little while, there's no sign of the sedan except the frame and a pile of parts, including the engine block and license plate. Oscar walks over to me with a bag. "We need to slag these, *mija*."

I take the bag from him. Inside is a collection of guns. I reach into my borrowed pants, pull out my pistol, and add it to the bag. I unlatch the welding rig, untangle the hoses, and thread a plasma torch onto it. I wheel the rig over to the mound of parts, dragging the bag along behind me.

I dump the guns onto the cement floor. The welding goggles create a smoky veil over everything until I flash the cutter and the tip boils to life with a white-hot point. I play the torch over the first pistol, heating up the grip and barrel to a cherry red and then squeeze the oxygen feed and cut into the hardened metal. The raspy hiss of the hot gasses fills my ears. I cut each gun and then apply the torch to the engine block, melting the vehicle identification number imprinted along the header. Moments later the license plate shrivels and melts onto the cement floor. Soon all the parts are just bits of slag. I flip my welding goggles down around my throat, and Oscar sprays the hot metal with a hose. The metal sizzles and twists in the cold water.

Oscar waves at me. "You're next. I need you clean."

What the hell is he talking about? He gestures at some shop coveralls in a heap near his feet. "I sent everyone home," he says. "I can leave too, if you want to do this alone."

Oh, right. I shrug. "*No me importa.*" I slip from my shirt and trousers, rotating in place as Oscar sprays me with water. His rough hand runs through my hair as he sluices the dried blood from my scalp. The cold water makes me shiver.

"*Que cagada!*"

He shakes his head. "*Mañana será otro día*, Reno. Just get through this night."

"*Estoy cansado de esta mierda,*" I spit as I pull on the shop coveralls. "Those fucking Russians won't live another week."

Oscar coils the hose. "Victor treats me well, but it's hard to grow old this way. I wish I had a simple life, *mija.*"

I hug him. "*Gracias*, Oscar. I'll always owe you."

He picks up my clothes and dumps them in the incinerator. "Do you want to stay here?"

"No, I have a place I'll go. I could use a ride though."

"Somewhere safe?"

"I think so."

He picks up the loose pieces of slagged gun and other assorted scrap. I help him carry it to the pile outside, some of the pieces still warm from the torch.

Afterward I direct him downtown. When he stops at a light, I quickly kiss him on the cheek and step out into the cool night.

"Thanks again, Oscar."

"*Vaya con Dios*, Reynosa."

He pulls away, leaving me alone on the street. The shop coveralls I wear smell like old paint and grease. The night breeze blows a shiver down my spine. I think of Roland at the bottom of the bay and shiver again. I press my hand against my mouth and close my eyes tight against the tears.

The dim glow of the moon shines on the sign for the Last Call. I rap on Jack's window. After a moment his face peeks between the curtains.

"Hi," I say weakly.

"Reno?"

"Can I come in?"

"Come around to the front."

He opens the door and I sag into him. "Are you okay?" he asks.

I nod into his chest and begin to cry. He strokes my hair as I shake in his arms. "What's wrong?" he asks in a hushed voice.

Once my crying subsides to sniffles, he gently eases me down the stairs and onto the bed. I curl into a ball and he pulls some covers over both of us. I snuggle against him and fall into a black sleep.

In the morning, I wake to find myself in bed with a shaft of sunlight coming through the simple curtains. Jack sits on the edge of a chair, sipping coffee and studying me.

"I was hoping you'd come by last night. I just didn't expect your visit would happen exactly like this." He hesitates. "Are you going to tell me what happened?"

"It's better if you don't know, trust me."

A brief flicker of irritation crosses his face. "You can ask for trust if you give it back. Roland said I had to earn your faith, but he didn't warn me it would be this hard just to get you to talk about your life. First you tell me you're a chocolate chef, but you're really a thief, and now you show up last night looking like you've been shot out of a cannon."

I press my lips together, but it's no use. Tears slip down my cheeks, and I swallow hard. "Roland's dead." Angrily wiping my eyes, I take a breath. "The Russians ambushed us. They killed Gartello and tried for Victor."

Jack sets his coffee cup on the table next to him. "Roland's dead?"

"Yeah, he's dead. And you want to know about my life? I can't ever relax and my friends all die. I might go to jail for a long time. I need to kill some people before they kill me. I can't ever sleep no matter how much I try." I explain how Carter's been blackmailing us—the tape, everything. He just listens as it all pours out of me.

He leans forward and takes my hand. "Oh, Reno," Jack whispers.

"Now the Russians are hunting me too."

"Over the caviar?"

"Yeah," I say, wiping my nose.

Jack lets out a long sigh. "Not just you then."

I realize he's right. Not just me and Victor. "I'm sorry I got you involved, Jack."

He shrugs. "That's mostly on Carter and Carmen. And me—I could have said no. You told me to stay out of it. And what are you going to do about Carter? You know he hasn't forgotten. He's just going to arrest you the day before."

"I don't know. I think maybe I'll kill him."

"No, I think we need him alive. We'll need his help against the Russians."

"How?"

Jack smiles.

July 19, 1986, 12:35 P.M.

"He said it wasn't dangerous."

I bounce the key in my palm and snap my gum while eyeballing the branch manager until he finally ambles over and escorts me into the vault with the safety deposit boxes.

I don't believe in ghosts. I've sent enough souls to their fate, and I figure any angry spirits would have made a point to visit me by now. Victor hasn't reported any poltergeists either, and his attic should be teeming with them. But it feels almost like Roland is standing next to me.

Surprisingly, the box is empty except for a pillowcase. I hoist it from the box and hear the rustle of cash. I still can't shake the feeling that Roland is with me as I carry it back to the sedan, newly delivered by Oscar. Probably stolen, and without my precious Lexan but better than nothing.

As I merge into traffic, I dump out the pillowcase. A couple bricks of cash and some jewelry spill onto the passenger seat.

I see a folded note in the cash and I open it up at the next stoplight.

To Whom It May Concern:

The contents of the safety deposit belong to my wife Angela Mouton as do all my other worldly belongings. In the event Angela Mouton cannot be located, I hereby appoint Reynosa Villarrubia as the sole executor of my estate to use her personal discretion as to the distribution of any and all of my worldly possessions.

Roland Mouton

There's a hastily scrawled postscript at the bottom:

Reno—If you're reading this, then I'm probably dead. If Angie cries when you tell her, let her know I loved her and that she was the one beautiful thing in my life. Tell her that even if she doesn't cry.

R

I wipe tears from my eyes and look out the window. A blaring horn startles me. I realize the light is green and gun the sedan across the intersection. Rolling down the window as I drive, I let the car fill with the rush of the wind.

I scoop the cash and jewelry back into the pillowcase when I reach Roland's building. As I trudge up the stairs to the apartment, I dig in my pocket for Roland's wedding ring and drop it into the pillowcase.

The building is nothing special, but the neighborhood is nice. Angie had almost certainly picked it out. Roland's tastes were definitely more street.

Holding the pillowcase in one hand, I knock on the door.

Angie answers, her brown hair piled into a loose bun on her head and mascara tears smudged on her cheeks. Her eyes dart past me, almost certainly looking for Roland. They flick back to me and her face crinkles in fear. "Where is Roland?" she asks. "Is he okay?"

"Can we talk inside?"

Angie puts her hand over her mouth and shudders with one huge gasping sob. I ease her back and step inside, swinging the door shut.

"Please tell me he's okay," she pleads. "He didn't come home. He didn't call. He always calls."

I take a breath. "He died last night, Angie. He got shot. I tried like hell to save him, but I couldn't do it." Tears fill my eyes too. They make Angie blurry, and it seems that my voice is a million miles away. "I really tried, Angie. I really did."

Angie leans into me, crying heavily. I smell the faint hint of lilac perfume on her cashmere sweater. In another room, I hear a baby start to wail. Angie wipes her cheeks with the heels of both hands.

"Just a second," she says and walks down the hallway.

I feel my sadness give way to anger like it always does. Even as Angie sobbed, my sadness was boiling away to leave a white-hot rock of fury toward Zhukov and Golnak.

Angie walks back into the room, the infant on her shoulder, lulling him back to sleep with pats to the back. She sits down on the couch. "Why would someone shoot Roland?"

I sit down next to her, setting the pillowcase on the floor. "I'm sorry, Angie, but I shouldn't tell you much." Angie's face hardens, and I reach out and touch her on the arm. "Because of what we do. The cops might come looking for you. The less you know, the better."

Angie hangs her head, her tears dimpling the wooden floor.

"Angie, look at me." She tilts her face toward me. "I talked to Roland before he died. He wanted you to know he loved you and that he wanted you to take care of yourself and the baby." I slide the bag over to her. "He wanted you to have this."

Angie nods, her lips quivering. The baby squirms in her lap. He reaches out and grabs my thumb. I let him pull it for a minute, enjoying the tug of his soft chubby fingers. "You should try to leave the city soon. Today, if you can."

Angie squints at me. "Why?"

"If anyone calls asking for him who you don't recognize, leave immediately," I continue. "If anyone knocks who you don't recognize, under no circumstances do you let them in, you understand?"

"Do people want to hurt me?"

I pause. "Angie, did Roland tell you what he did for a living?"

"A little. He said you two were like bodyguards, but that it was mostly just driving around. He said it wasn't dangerous." Fresh tears run down her cheeks. One drips onto the baby's head, and he rubs at it curiously.

"The people who killed Roland don't know he's dead. They might still be looking for him. If they find you, they'll hurt you to get at him."

"What did Roland do to make them so mad?"

I swallow. "He saved my life. I tried to save his, I swear to God, but he got shot up too bad."

Angie begins to sob again.

I stand up. "Angie, I'm sorry. I should go now." I walk to the door.

Angie calls out to me. When I turn, she flashes me a sad smile. "He talked about you a lot. He really liked you, you know that?"

I sit in the car afterward and stare out the passenger window. The baby looks like him. I can still feel the touch of his hand on mine. I can't remember the last time I touched anything that pure.

May 19, 1973, 2:56 p.m.

"You can have anything."

I dump a handful of cigarette butts onto the soiled carpet. Miguel glances at my treasure, his hands never stopping their intricate dance as he splices bits of rope into one strand. Bits of rope are worthless, but an entire strand had value. His long hair is gathered into a ponytail and bound by a rubber band.

"Marlboro?" he eventually grunts.

I nod. Of course Marlboro. Miguel had strict rules when it came to what he called cigarette recovery. Only Marlboro, and only filterless. It had taken me weeks to learn the differences between the various cigarettes.

"*Bueno.* Sit with me a moment, *mija.*" He puts aside his rope and we both begin unrolling the cigarettes, creating a mound of brown tobacco between us.

"It's time for you to go into the city and work with Pablo." He looks at me, his eyes bright and focused. Grime permanently dulls everything in the *favela*, but his eyes stay bright and clean. "You must be careful. Listen to Pablo, do what he says."

I nod.

Miguel hesitates, then slides a hand beneath his

blue-turned-to-brown poncho and pulls a sheaf of rolling papers from his pants pocket. His tongue darts out, moistening the edge of the paper, and his clever hands quickly roll a perfect cigarette. "You must dress a certain way," he continues. "Big trousers, big shirt. Nothing tight. And boots. Wear thick boots."

I scowl at that. "I don't like shoes."

Miguel holds up a finger. "Listen to me. Once you leave here, you become just another *desechable*. Do you know what that means? Disposable. Trash. Nothing. Wearing boots is a way to hide your weakness. Never let them know that you're weak."

He withdraws a match from his pocket and lights his cigarette. For just a brief flash, his face creases into a smile.

"Is that all?"

"No." He takes another drag, and then pulls from his pocket what looks like a black handle of some sort. He holds it up. "This is a knife. If you press your thumb like this, then you have a blade." He grip tightens and suddenly a blade flicks open from the side of the handle.

I jump.

Miguel laughs. He folds the blade back into the handle and hands it to me.

"Careful." He places my hand against the side, away from a slit that runs the length of it. "Hold it so the blade can flick outward."

It feels smooth and heavy and dangerous in my hand. I fearfully press the button, and the blade flicks out like a tongue of a snake. The blade glitters. I love it.

"Can I have it?"

"Maybe a trade," Miguel says, his eyebrows raised.

"Anything," I say quickly.

"You don't know what I want."

I don't care. But I have nothing to give except cigarettes. Maybe my belt? I would just find another. "You can have anything."

Miguel extends his hand. "Give me the knife."

My heart sinks. I reluctantly drop the knife into his open hand.

Miguel looks into me with his eyes bright. "Anything?"

I nod.

Miguel stands up. "On your feet and turn around."

Confused and a little scared, I stand up and do what he asks. Miguel had always been kind to me, but I can't help but remember Reuben and fear starts to fill me.

I feel Miguel's hand on my neck, slowly rising into my hair. I hear the *snick* of the blade opening.

The blade presses up against my neck, the steel a cold line. Miguel gathers my hair into a knot in his fist.

I pull away, but he has me tight.

I feel the blade slice through my hair.

My hands instinctively go to the back of my neck, strangely cool now in the air.

"Why did you do that?" I protest.

Miguel folds the blade back and hands the knife to me. "Our trade. You said anything, so I took your hair."

"Why?"

Miguel spins me around. "Reynosa, you must not look like a woman on the streets. You must become just another grubby boy with boots who is on his way to his job. You wear a hat, you look at the ground, and you never call attention to yourself." He lifts his hand, my hair dangling like a shiny black snake. "No beautiful hair, no curves, nothing that will bring you trouble." He puts his hand on my shoulder. "Maybe someday you can let it grow back but for now you hide, listen to Pablo, and stay out of trouble, *si*?"

July 21, 1986, 4:52 P.M.

"And I need an organ myself."

I circle the block a couple of times, sniffing for tails or anything that looks wrong. Victor's slumped in the back seat, glaring out the window. I ease through an alley and stop at the back entrance to Gotelli's Tattoo Parlor.

I let the car idle. "We shouldn't be here."

"Relax," Victor says. "A public hit's not Zhukov's style. He's too sneaky. Plus you probably killed half his crew last week. Everyone is taking a break."

"You sure Carter said Gotelli's?"

"Yeah."

"Why?"

Victor shrugs. "He didn't elaborate."

"I'd really like to kill that bastard."

"Today you just relax," Victor says. "You'll be free tomorrow."

"You really think he'll just let it go?"

"Actually, no, I don't but if Jack's plan unfolds as you say, I think Carter will forget all about it."

When Jack had revealed his plan, I felt like my body was

a balloon filled with helium. I practically levitated off his bed. "Oh, yes. Jack's idea is excellent."

"So today you just relax. Wait for tomorrow."

So I take a breath, try to relax, fail miserably, and walk into the tattoo parlor. The smell of hot ink and the buzz of needles fill the space. Gotelli's specializes in dancers. Several of the girls are topless, eyes closed tight against the pain as the needle hums across the curves of their breasts.

Carter is talking to a lithe blonde who lies on her stomach while the needle draws a dragon crawling down the small of her back, its green tongue flicking down the cleft of her ass. Carter looks up and smirks when he sees me.

"You want to get inked, Reno? I can get it done on the house."

I ignore him and scan the room for threats. I don't see any signs of ambush and step aside for Victor to enter the room.

Carter herds us into the manager's office, a small room with a pane of glass in the wall so he can see the working room. "Any sign of my gun?" Carter asks as he closes the door.

"No," Victor says. "I wanted to ask you to not visit the shop any more. You and your partner upset Cora. She said he was very rude."

Carter shrugs. "Chief made Larry a special investigator on gun crimes, assigned me to him. Old fucker might forget his glasses or when to take his pills, but he's the lead and I gotta follow where he goes. I don't have any leverage on him."

Victor purses his lips and nods. "Indeed. Your new partner—what's his name again?"

"Larry Holland. I'm sure you'll meet him yourself soon."

"Do you think I can buy him off? Make him forget us?"

He shakes his head. "He forgets lots of things, but not you. He told the chief that you're fencing guns, and he won't give up till you're convicted."

"Why so much interest? We haven't handled weapons in a long time."

"Old case. One of his friends was murdered a few years back, probably by Chopek."

Victor raises his eyebrows. "What else?"

Carter lowers his voice. "Hey, that was a huge clusterfuck over at Gartello's the other night. You guys gotta keep it down." He shakes his head. "Way, way too many dead Russians. I thought Gartello was going to smooth things out, not get wacked." He removes his inhaler from his jacket and raises it in my direction, as if toasting me. "And you, little lady, have quite the mean streak. Zhukov's going to funerals every day this week."

"Roland didn't make it," I say.

He shrugs at me and looks back at Victor.

"Did you hear me?" I hiss. I want to dig my fingers into his throat and choke him to death. "Roland's dead. And it's your fault."

Carter snorts. "You're telling me that all that shit went down because of fish eggs?" he says to Victor. "No way. You and Zhukov been screwing with each other for years, Victor. Just a matter of time before something like this happened." He arches his eyebrows. "Even old man Gartello didn't like the shit you were pulling. The only surprise was Gartello eating bullets too. Zhukov's the man now."

Victor frowns. "Maybe Zhukov suspected I had interfered with his operations occasionally, but it would be difficult for him to prove anything."

I suddenly feel old. How did it get to this? Arguing fault with a degenerate cop? Victor should have never allowed us to be blackmailed. He should have told me. I would have left and none of this would have happened.

Carter shakes his head. "Zhukov didn't need proof."

"He couldn't prove anything until you botched the caviar job," Victor replies. "After that, he must have connected the dots."

"Zhukov connected your dots a long time ago, trust me. Just a matter of time."

"Carter, you listen—"

"No, you listen! Yeah, the job went shitty, but you were playing with fire for years, Victor. Those Russians are fucked-up crazy. You're lucky only that dumbass Roland bought it. You should have all died in that room."

A little thread in my heart snaps. I pull the switchblade from my boot, flick open the blade, and slide the point right up against Carter's pupil. "If you had done your job, none of this would have happened. It was your fuck-up that got us into this, so you're going to help us, Carter, or so help me I'll—"

Carter is unimpressed. "What? Kill me? You're going to kill a federal agent? With your badass little knife?"

"Reno…" Victor says softly.

"You're a piece of shit," I hiss at Carter.

Carter shakes his head. "Yeah, I'm the one to blame. You don't get it." He glances out the window. "Hey, do me a favor for once and get the doctor in here, okay? Is that too much to ask?" He points to the front of the parlor, where Dr. Barrington is peering around the room. What the hell is he doing here?

I flick the blade back into the handle and give Carter a venomous look before stalking out the door.

"Hey, Doc," I say.

He whirls around so suddenly he stumbles. I put out a hand to steady him. "Hello, Reno," he says, blinking at me in surprise.

"What are you doing here?" I ask.

"Special Agent Carter wanted to meet."

"You?"

He nods. "He called me this morning," he says miserably. He blinks a couple more times and looks at his watch. "Excuse me—he told me not to be late."

Why would Carter call Barrington? I don't know, but I doubt it's going to be a happy moment for the doctor. I follow him into the manager's office.

"Hey, Doc, glad you could make it," Carter says.

Barrington grimaces. "I can't meet like this. Somebody will notice."

"Nobody's gonna notice anything, Doc. They got their minds on other things."

Barrington glances at a half-naked stripper on a table outside the room, the tattoo artist swirling an intricate sun and moon pattern around her crotch. "I shouldn't be here," he says again.

"You got the stuff?" asks Carter.

Barrington looks away from the stripper, trying to find a place for his gaze. I see he doesn't want to look at Carter and he shrinks from Victor too. In the end, he just sticks out his hand almost blindly and hands Carter a brown envelope.

Carter opens it, and I watch him fan a sheaf of what looks like prescriptions. "Good work, Doc. But I'm going to need more."

"What?" Barrington squawks, finally looking Carter in

the face. "You said just this once. I can't keep doing this. It's against the law."

Carter squints at him. "What?"

Barrington folds his hands across his chest. "I'm not going to do it. I can't. I could lose my license."

"Don't worry about losing your job when you could lose a lot more, Doc. You're an accessory after the fact, aiding felons, concealing a crime—I could go on."

"Why am I here, Carter?" asks Victor tiredly.

"What's the market price for a good liver?" Carter asks Barrington.

"They're not for sale. You can't buy them."

"Doc, I've been patiently waiting in line for years, but now they say I'm not a good candidate. You're telling me that with life or death on the line, people won't sell?"

"Yes, that's what I'm telling you. But if a relative or friend wants to volunteer an organ then usually something can be arranged."

"He doesn't have friends," I say.

Carter ignores me. "Doc, I'm what you could call a student of human nature. See I'm convinced that with a little help from you, all of us could make a good business of this, and I could get what I need too."

Barrington shakes his head. "I don't see how I can help you."

"Ah, Doc, you're so wrong. You just need to provide me the transplant list, contact information for each person, plus the organ they're waiting for. I'll make the introductions myself. Victor will be in charge of, um, collecting the organs. You just take care of the doctor part."

"I won't do that," Barrington says. I can hear the shock in his voice. "You're going to extort those people."

"Like I said earlier, you shouldn't worry too much about that license. Besides, we'll be helping people. I thought you would like that aspect."

Barrington looks around the room with a look of pleading resignation. "What did I do to you people?" he asks quietly. "I just tried to save your friend."

A wave of sadness washes through me. I'm reminded of Roland, of holding his hand when he died. Tears form in my eyes, creating a corona around everything in the room.

"Doc, I'm very motivated on this subject," Carter says. "Are you hearing me?"

"You'd need a whole surgical team," Barrington sighs. "And I don't know anything about transplants."

"But you have friends, right?"

"Carter, why am I here?" Victor asks again. "I've got business elsewhere."

"I have a special surprise for you both," Carter snaps, "especially for Reno. But that'll have to wait for tomorrow. I have a more pressing topic today. I think we should be in the organ collection business. I talk to the customers, you collect from the donors." He smiles at me. "And with your little attack dog here, I doubt there'll be any shortage of organs."

I suddenly notice that Barrington is leaning to one side. I put out a hand to steady him just as he faints, toppling onto Carter and sending them both crashing to the floor.

"Damn it!" Carter pushes Barrington off of him and lurches clumsily to his feet. "What the hell is wrong with you?"

"Too much for him," I say. "I don't blame him. You're an asshole." I help Barrington up. "Let's get some air, Doc. I'll walk you back to your car." He clings to me as I help him out the door and through the parlor.

In the parking lot Barrington steps away from me and rubs his nose. He's not looking at anything and I can tell he's trying to regain his composure.

"Don't worry about Carter too much," I say. "I have a feeling he won't be bugging you again, okay?"

"Leave me alone."

I follow him to a dirty Volvo. He drops his keys. When he bends down to retrieve them he crumples against the tire.

Another wave of sadness grips me. He looks so miserable. "Come by Victor's office in a couple days, okay? I'll give you back your pictures. We won't bother you anymore."

He looks at me, hope filling his face. "Really?"

"Really."

"What about Carter?"

"Don't worry about Carter, Doc. I have a feeling he'll have a change of heart in a couple of days."

July 22, 1986, 10:16 A.M.

"Ever think you'd get shot dead by your own gun?"

I stir the chocolate, letting the surface almost wrinkle before stirring again. I drop in a little more butter and mix it in, turning down the gas burner just a bit. I keep nervously glancing at the clock, waiting for Carter to show up and wondering where Jack is.

Victor sits at Cora's cooling table reviewing his pen pal letters. This is his favorite day of the week. His sponsored girls send him weekly letters telling him about their lives, the sweet triumphs and bitter defeats that flavor their days. Some are in crayon, some in ink. Many include drawings or small gifts. Victor treasures them all.

Occasionally Cora ventures back into the kitchen and chides me. "Keep the heat low, dear. Just enough. I can't have even a tiny bit of scalding."

I just nod and stir vigorously. My policy is to never argue with Cora about chocolate.

"Not too fast," Cora laughs. "You'll emulsify the chocolate. Just keep the heat low and stir evenly."

I nod again. Quick enough to keep the chocolate from

burning but slow enough to keep air from foaming it. Just right.

The bell on the door tinkles and Cora hurries to the front. Moments later I hear Carter's rough laughter. A tiny tremor runs up my spine and adrenaline floods my body. I can taste fear like gasoline on my tongue and take a breath to steady myself. Nothing to worry about.

Carter walks into the room. "I was hoping to find you here."

I hear the door jingle again. A few moments later Jack walks into the kitchen. A ripple of unease briefly flickers across Carter's face.

"Hey, Jack," Carter says. "What the fuck are you doing here?"

Jack sits down at the table with Victor. "I want to know how you're going to help Carmen."

Carter shakes his head. "I'm not."

Jack stares back at him.

"Look, Jack, the DA has filed about a dozen charges against her." Carter looks at the ceiling and counts on his fingers as he speaks. "Robbery, murder, resisting arrest, grand theft, and a bunch of other stuff. There's no way she'll qualify for bail and her sentence should be something like sixty years to life—maybe a death sentence if she gets the wrong jury. Not much I can do."

Jack shrugs. "You need to find a way. For your own sake."

"I don't think I like your attitude," Carter says with a brittle smile.

Jack looks like he's going to rip the bastard apart. "*My* attitude? You were the arresting officer! Your man went berserk and killed a guy! The same guy that you said wasn't going to be there in the first place!"

Carter waves his hand. "We're off-topic anyway. I have a little guessing game I want to play with you all. We'll start easy." He gets up from the table, walks over to me, dips his finger in my chocolate pot, and sucks on it. "Hmmm, you always have the best candy, Reno, you know that?"

I throw the spoon into the sink and snap off the gas. "You just ruined the batch. I can guess where that finger's been."

"I know where you want it."

"Carter, what do you want?" Victor interrupts.

"What day is it?" he replies innocently.

"Wednesday."

"And the significance of today?" Carter prompts.

Victor taps his finger on one of his chins. "I don't have any idea. Reno, anything come to mind?"

I wipe my hands on my apron. "No idea."

"You of all people should know, Reno." Carter slips his handcuffs from his coat pocket and wiggles them at me. "Maybe these will give you a hint."

I shake my head. "Still doesn't mean anything to me."

"Does 'statute of limitations' mean anything to you? It's almost expired." He smiles. "But not completely. This is the last day, actually."

I untie my apron and let it fall to the floor. "You were never going to let it go, were you?"

"I thought about it, but you're such a bitch that, no, I couldn't let it go. I'm taking you to jail for arson and while it won't do much for my career, it'll be a personal highlight."

"I have a game too," Jack says. "I want to play show and tell."

Carter scratches his ear and considers Jack for a moment.

"Jack, you're starting to irritate me. Maybe I should arrest you too. You and Carmen can both spend the rest of your lives in jail."

Jack pulls out a pistol from his waistband and aims it at Carter.

"What the hell are you doing? You're going to shoot me?"

Jack grins. "That's a good idea, but no. Don't you recognize this gun?"

Carter freezes for a moment as slow realization compresses his lips into a thin white line. I see hatred redden his face like there's magma moving below the surface of his skin. His eyes bulge and he takes a long hit from his inhaler. "You fucking cocksucker," he finally wheezes.

"Ever think you'd get shot dead by your own gun?" Jack asks.

"That could be anybody's," Carter sputters. "You're bluffing."

Jack shrugs. "Yeah, I guess so. If you can't identify it, maybe police ballistics could help us."

"I shouldn't have waited," he hisses at me. "I should have never even thought about waiting. I should have busted you the moment I could."

I smile, savoring the moment.

"What now?" Carter asks.

"We have some requests. Small favors," Jack says.

Carter sighs. "Of course you do."

"Get Carmen out," Jack says. "And do it quick."

"And we need some help with some Russians," I say.

I watch Carter's mouth open and closing like a dying fish's.

Victor laughs. It's the first time I've heard him laugh in many years.

May 19, 1973, 5:56 P.M.

"I'll call you Reno, okay?"

The next morning, I meet Pablo. He inspects me with a puzzled frown. "What happened to your hair?"

"Miguel cut it."

Pablo circles me, staring intently. "He isn't much of a barber. Looks like he used a knife."

I'm suddenly embarrassed. "He wants me to look like a boy."

"If you keep the hat low, nobody can tell. But Reynosa is a girl's name. When we're in the city, we have to use something else. I'll call you Reno, okay?"

"Whatever." I stand on one foot and jiggle my new switchblade in my boot. "What are we going to do? Collect cigarettes?"

"That's for little kids. You're with me now. Just follow."

We wind down narrow trails through the mounds of garbage and shanties, Pablo occasionally waving to kids blackened by a life in mud and neglect. I ignore everyone and just follow, wondering exactly where we're going.

Pablo stops at a tin shack near the beach. A white-haired woman answers his knock. "Yes?"

"*Hola*, Amelia," Pablo says to her. "I need a suit and a hat that matches."

Now it's Pablo's turn for inspection. "*Por Dios*, you're filthy," says Amelia. Her face is wrinkled and bronzed like a walnut shell, but she strikes me as amazingly clean, the cleanest person I've seen since I arrived in Cartagena. "Wait here." She disappears into the darkness of her shack and returns a moment later with a small bar of soap. "Take this, go to the beach, don't come back until you're clean."

Pablo frowns. "Just give me the suit."

"Do as I say, then you'll get what you need. Go on."

"*Puta*," Pablo says under his breath but spins on his heel and marches off.

"Put some of that soap in your mouth!" she calls after him.

Pablo raises his middle finger behind him as he stomps away.

"And what do you want?" Amelia asks me.

"Nothing," I reply, my eyes on the ground just like Miguel told me.

She takes my chin in her hand and gently lifts my head. Her expression changes from puzzlement to concern. "You fooled me for a moment. I thought you were just another filthy boy."

I say nothing.

"Are your parents here?"

I shrug.

"If you need anything, you come here, okay?"

I look in her face and see a simple, genuine kindness. A sad smile raises a couple dimples and I catch a glimmer of what remains of her beauty. She runs her hand through my coarse-cut hair. "Wait here," she says. Her hand was warm and soft, and I can still feel its touch after it's gone.

A moment later she returns with a pair of scissors. "Do you mind? I can give you a proper boy haircut, I think." She moves around me, a soft hand on my shoulder occasionally as her scissors click and snip. She murmurs a little song as she works. My black hair drops in small clumps around me like leaves from a tree. A sense of peace fills me that had been lost for a long time.

Pablo returns about five minutes later, wet and dressed only in his shorts. He silently regards us for a moment, then angrily announces, "Okay, I'm clean. Give me the clothes!"

Amelia ignores him, continuing with my haircut as Pablo glowers. "Much better! Still a boy, but more presentable." She turns to Pablo. "What do you have to say to me now?"

"My suit. Bring it to me."

"What else?"

Pablo looks mystified. "And my hat?"

"And an apology."

"For what?"

Irritation deepens the creases on Amelia's face. "Just because we live in a *favela* doesn't mean we have no manners, Pablo. You know why you owe me an apology."

Amelia had awoken something in me. A sense of myself, of someone who matters. How long had it been since I was dumped here in the garbage? A month? A year? I don't know. Just a blur of collecting trash, eating things that other people wouldn't, collecting cigarette butts for the one person in the world who didn't make me beg.

"Apologize to her, Pablo," I say.

Pablo stares at me with a look of amazement that slowly fades to resignation. "I'm sorry I swore at you," he says to Amelia. "It was wrong." He gives a ridiculous bow in his wet underwear. "But can you please give me the fucking clothes so we can get going?"

"Yes, you'll get your suit and hat and also something for your, um, brother." Once more Amelia darts into her shack and this time retrieves a brown canvas suit on a hanger with a matching brown handkerchief. "Try not to get it too dirty or rip it, Pablo."

"Gracias," he says flatly.

Amelia hands him an old green felt hat that more or less fits and a red bandana for me. "Be careful. Blood leaves stains."

July 24, 1986, 5:33 P.M.

"You need to be dead for lots of reasons."

As I approach my Ducati, I see a guy in a gray suit kneeling near it. Larry Holland. I tip-toe up to him. My switchblade makes a quiet click and then the blade is at his throat.

He stiffens, then both hands slowly go up. "I'm a special agent with the FBI," he says slowly. "I'm going to reach into my jacket and show you my badge, okay?"

"I know who you are. I remember your little visit to the chocolate shop."

I snap the blade back and let him stand up.

He sticks out his hand. "Sorry about that. Let's start over. My name's Larry."

I ignore the gesture. "You should be more careful. This isn't a good neighborhood. You could get hurt." I nod at the black disk in his left hand. "What's that?"

He holds it up. "This? Oh, just a fancy radio. Just to keep in touch with the precinct."

I scoff. "Really? It's not a transponder?"

"Well, actually, yes," he says after a moment. "I'm not a very good liar, I guess."

"I think you're probably a very good liar, Larry."

He smiles. "Okay, Reno, yes."

I cock my head. "Yes?"

He shrugs. "Yes to everything. Yes, I'm a good liar. Yes, I was planting a tracking beacon, and yes, I'm investigating you for a variety of crimes." He holds up the transponder and turns it in his hand. "I've spent some time following you, trying to understand you, and now I'm afraid I screwed everything up and won't be able to help you."

"Help me do what? You don't know anything about me."

"Actually, I know a lot about you. Age twenty-five, bodyguard and killer for Victor Pagnolli, born in… where? I forget."

"Colombia," I say.

He snaps his fingers. "That's right! I always confuse the countries down there. While I don't know this for a fact, I think you were involved in a hit on another bad man named Zhukov. You're just one unlucky break from being killed or arrested." He smiles at me. "So you see, I know a lot."

I raise an eyebrow. "Yeah, you're a genius." I step past him and straddle the bike, inserting the key into the ignition.

He puts his hand over mine. "Reno, you have a choice. You don't need to go down with Pagnolli. It is only a matter of time. You can choose to walk away. You've got skills. You're fluent in Spanish, and my files say that you're more than qualified to teach self-defense. You could go back to Colombia. Or there's always immunity…"

"Thanks for the advice, Larry. Now go to hell." I turn the key and rev the engine.

"Think about it, Reno," he shouts over the roar of the motorcycle. "Get out while you can!"

I gun the engine and spin the rear wheel. Larry jumps

back and I rocket out of the alley, punching through the gears and weaving through traffic until I get to the Sweet Tooth.

When I arrive, Jack is waiting there along with Carter and Victor.

Jack greets me with a hug. Carter gives me his usual shitty smirk.

"I met your partner again," I say to Carter. "He's not like you. He might actually try to do the right thing and solve crimes."

"Very funny," Carter says. "Larry's a pain in the ass, but he isn't our main problem right now. Our old pal Carmen has had a change of heart. Watch this."

Carter pops a tape into our VHS player. He presses play, and I see Carmen slumped on a metal chair in what looks like an interrogation room. I shiver like someone is walking over my grave.

Carmen touches her swollen eye, perhaps probing for an infection. A female guard holding a baton stands near the door.

On the video, I see the door open. Carter walks in, looking vaguely sad and distracted, followed closely by Larry Holland. Carter's face remains slack despite Carmen's surprised look.

The guard puts her baton under Carmen's chin. "I'll be right outside," she says. "Don't get any stupid ideas."

After the guard leaves, Larry straddles a chair across from her. "So, you killed Ivan Chopek, eh?" he asks cheerfully. "I should shake your hand. He needed to get killed a long time ago."

Carmen shrugs. "Who are you guys?"

"My name is Larry Holland, and my partner here is Carter Hansen. We're both with the FBI."

"What do you want?"

"Carmen, you're a smart lady," Larry replies. "You know what we want, and we know what you want."

"You know a lot, I guess."

Larry smiles. "We want Victor Pagnolli, and you want to get the hell out of here."

"What makes you think I can get you Pagnolli?" she says. "Or would want to?"

Larry squints at her. "Carmen, I think you and I could be friends, but you have to stop acting stupid. You worked with Chopek, and Chopek worked for Pagnolli. I know this, and so do you." He stands up and holds up a finger. "If it were just us, I think it could be our little secret, but sadly for you a really bad man named Anatoli Zhukov knows that you tried to rip him off."

Carmen just stares at him, saying nothing.

Larry points to her cut eye. "It looks like you've already made the acquaintance of some of Zhukov's people on the inside." He shrugs. "I'm trying to think why Zhukov would let you live much longer than a week. Or Pagnolli, for that matter. You need to be dead for lots of reasons. So when you ask me a question like why do I think you can get me Pagnolli, I think you're either stupid or you think I'm stupid."

Carmen purses her lips and looks at the ceiling.

Larry leans across the table. "Carmen, I'm not kidding you. You're not going to make it through the week. You need to think very clearly about your options."

"We could probably get you into a safe house," Carter

says, "maybe witness protection, but you have to give us something in return."

Carmen gives him an evil grin. "I've got something better than Pagnolli."

Larry sits back. "Oh? Like what?"

"Yeah, okay, I know some bad guys. And some of those guys belong to you."

Larry raises his eyebrows. "Come again?"

"I know some dirty cops. You should clean you own house first, don't you think?"

"Bullshit."

"If you get me in protective custody, I can give you a bad cop *and* Pagnolli," she says. "You'll be able to connect the dots from there. If I can't, I'm dead like you say but if I'm right, I get into witness protection."

Jack leans forward and presses pause. "You were supposed to explain things to her! You were supposed to tell her you were going to help her out."

Carter takes a breath. "I *did* explain it to her, you fucktard. Just watch. It gets better. Your old girlfriend or whatever the fuck she is, is really going to screw us all." Carter looks like he's starting to rot, like a day-old fish. I'm beginning to feel the same way. He presses play again and sits back as the tape rolls again.

"Look, Carmen, you can give us Pagnolli or you can go back to your little party back in the hole," Carter snaps. "Don't try to con us with dirty cops and connecting dots."

Larry holds up his hand. "Let me get this straight. You're telling me that cops are mixed up with Pagnolli—and what? A murder?"

Carmen shrugs. "Get me out of here first."

"She's a lying sack of shit, Larry," Carter says. "Let's go, she's wasting our time."

Larry regards Carmen for a moment. "No, I think this is worth pursuing. We'll put you in a safe house until we can figure something out. But the DA will need some sweetening before we can arrange the paperwork."

"I'll be sweet as sugar if you get me out of here," she says.

"Just sit tight," he says. "Don't do anything irreversible, you follow me? It ain't too late for you."

Carter presses stop and leans back in his chair. "I *did* explain it to Carmen. I made it very clear. She knew what to say to get her into a safe house. She went off script. I think she blames you for almost getting her stabbed to death, Vic."

"She's just making up a story, guaranteeing she's got enough to trade," Jack says. "She won't rat us out. Just get her into a house and it will go as planned."

"No, let's just finish the job," Victor grunts. "If she's going to talk, best to silence her now."

"Agreed," I say.

"No. We're not killing her," Jack says.

"Not smart," Victor says. "She dealt the hand. Either she does exactly what she's told, or she has to go."

I look at Jack, wondering what he's thinking. I can never tell… I can't read his face, and I can't help thinking about him and Carmen. He didn't tell me that he had Carter's gun or that he even knew Carter. A little shiver of fear runs through me, and I think that maybe I don't know Jack at all.

"Whatever," Carter says bitterly. "Jack's got the gun, Jack's the boss." He puts his hands over his face and slides them down with a heavy breath. "What a clusterfuck. I'll talk to her again, make sure she stays patient."

Victor shoots me a glance. At least I know what *he's* thinking. Kill them both right now, finish Carmen later. Don't rely on either to help us against the Russians. Simplify.

Silence fills the room. Victor keeps staring at me. I look away with a small shake of my head.

"You mentioned something about Zhukov and a funeral?" I say to Carter.

July 26, 1986, 11:53 A.M.

"Scared?"

"It's too risky," Jack says as he picks the lock on my apartment door.

"No risk, no reward," I reply.

"Too soon." He jiggles the pick. "Feeling the spring tension on the tumblers," he adds.

I nod like I know what he's talking about. "Last funeral. Last chance." I lean over him, inspecting his operation on the my doorknob. "Harder than you thought, huh?"

"Easier. Only four tumblers and loose too."

He gently slides his pick a little and my door lock releases with a click. He laughs at the surprise on my face.

"Pay up," he says and walks into my living room, which still looks like a gymnasium that collided with a Japanese tatami room. Barbells and various exercise pads clutter the floor and I'm suddenly very conscious of how weird it looks. He wanders over to examine some photographs on my living room wall. He points to an old Polaroid.

"You look scared. Who's the boy?"

"A friend." Pablo.

"None of your parents?"

"They're all lost. I think about my dad every day though."

"I wish he were here," he says. "Maybe he could change your mind about this crazy plan."

I grab his hand. "You don't have to go with me. Oscar would help."

"I doubt that. He has more sense. You don't owe this to Roland, you know. I bet if we talk to Zhukov, let him know we were forced into it by Carter, he would back off, especially since he can have whatever he wants right now."

Roland's name brings a surge of anger and I drop Jack's hand. "Are you crazy? If Zhukov ever sees my face again, I'm dead."

Jack nods glumly. "Okay. Then let's just leave town."

"Now, or after we get Carmen out?" I ask, knowing the answer.

"Reno, I owe her."

I look away, wondering again about Jack.

"Even if you don't trust me," he says, "understand that I'm in as deep with the Russians as you are."

I can almost hear Roland saying that I need to trust someone. "I understand. Let's just take care of Zhukov either way."

We drive across town and walk into the funeral home. I sit next to Jack in the back row and watch a Chinese family grieve the passing of a loved one. A line forms so they can pay the widow and her daughters their respects.

"I'll be right back," Jack says.

He smiles at everyone as he marches past the coffin and ducks behind the curtains. I feel a little foolish and out of place alone on the pew, so I wander around the facility looking for signs of alarms or even cameras. Nothing obvious. Of course, what would you steal from a funeral home?

A man with an ancient face asks me in accented English for the location of the men's room. Thanks to my quick tour, I'm able to point it out and the man nods in thanks before he ambles off.

I answer the same question several times, each time nodding somberly at the request and pointing the way. A steady stream of Chinese men with swollen bladders proceeds down the hall. After a while, I get the distinct impression that they think I work for the funeral home.

Eventually, Jack comes back, hooks my arm through his, and we march out just as the service ends. Owl-eyed old men stare at us in surprise as we leave.

"What are they looking at?" Jack whispers.

"It would be hard to explain. Where did you go?"

"Back room. I pretended I was lost. It looks pretty simple—they just load the casket into an elevator leading down to the garage and slide it directly into the hearse. It's the only place to make the switch. Looks like a two-man job, counting the driver."

"It'll be easy," I say.

He shakes his head. "Sure. What could go wrong?"

Once outside, I smile at the last few old men. I wonder what my father would have looked like in his old age. Would we recognize each other now? Maybe he's with my mother now, happy finally.

"See the driver near the hearse?" I say out the side of my mouth to Jack. "Just a plain black suit. We'll grab his cap, put some shades on you, and nobody will know the difference."

"Brilliant," he says sarcastically.

I smirk at him. "Scared?"

He nods. "Yeah, I think that adequately describes my feelings. This plan is nuts and so am I for going along with it."

I punch him in the arm. "Big baby. Come on, let's get you a suit."

July 27, 1986, 4:32 A.M.

"Roland would have approved."

The next morning, so early we're using flashlights, Jack cracks an old Schlage as easily as he had picked my apartment lock, and we creep into the funeral home's garage. An old black hearse squats on its wheels, empty for now. I nod toward a dilapidated shed filled with spades and ropes. Carrying my satchel, I shuffle into the shed with Jack and close the doors.

He watches me tear off strips of duct tape and arrange plastic tie straps. "We'll wait until the driver is almost ready to go," I say.

He just shakes his head.

I hum as I arrange the strips of duct tape. I open my satchel again and pull out the guns. Two Uzis, double-clipped with no harness or butt. The snub-nosed guns clink softly as I check safeties and secure the clips.

"What if someone finds us?"

I purse my lips. "You mean like four or five armed Russian thugs, who happen to know we're in here and want to shoot this shed up?"

"I'm serious. I don't like guns. This isn't what I do."

"I know. Does it bother you that I dropped Chopek?"

He closes his eyes. "That was different."

"How?"

He lets out his breath with a slow sigh. "He was going to kill that little girl. I dream about it. All kinds of different ways. Sometimes I kill Chopek myself, but lots of times I miss, and he shoots me. Once I pulled the trigger, but I accidentally shot you."

"Just dreams, Jack," I say, squeezing his arm. "I'm glad I shot him. The guy was an asshole. Look, if things go shitty here, follow my lead. If I start shooting, stay behind me. We'll go straight out the way we came. If you get shot, keep moving. It'll hurt like hell, but you have to keep going, no matter much it hurts."

"Lovely plan. I've already memorized it."

We spend the next couple of hours sitting, cramped and cold, occasionally talking although Jack seems content to sit quietly. Just as he finally asks how long I think we'll spend trapped in the shed, I hear keys jingle.

The entrance door to the garage squeaks open, and footsteps echo against the cement walls. I wait, filled with a sudden dread that the shed door will open and I will see Golnak holding a gun. But a moment later I can smell that it's just the flowers arriving. A twenty-minute interval of silence ensues, and then the harsh bark of Russian fills the air. The floor above us creaks as people began to arrive for the funeral service.

Alternating bouts of calm and panic sweep through me. For a while, I almost doze, but then I become tense, hands clenched into my knees. For his part, Jack just sits quietly.

My thoughts meander. I remember when Roland and I were traveling through New Mexico, where we drank tequila and I learned about lizard tamales and a Navajo game with a name I couldn't pronounce. Roland lost a whole lot of money. More, in fact, than he had in his possession. That awkward situation forced us to leave the game prematurely, steal a car, puke somewhere in the Taos desert, and finally end up at a hotel near Houston. A few hours later, eight pissed-off Navajo Indians broke in and beat the hell out of both of us. They stole Roland's belt buckle, two shotguns, and his boots. I almost giggle at the memory of Roland standing in his socks watching the Indians drive away with his stolen car.

After a while, I begin slowly flexing my arms. I pick up both Uzis and begin a methodical pantomime. Swivel, extend, rotate, squat, and then another swivel. Piece of cake. I smile at Jack and notice the sweat on his temple.

"You okay?" I whisper.

He nods, looking at the shovels covered with dried mud. They smell of musty dirt, of the grave. He jumps when the organ music starts up.

I lay the Uzi aside, double-check the strips of tape, and grin at him. "Remember—tape the mouths and eyes in that order, then the hands and legs. Just roll it around. Don't be neat. We'll only have a minute or so."

Jack nods again, and I wonder if he's going to be okay. He looks sick. A few moments later, I hear snatches of Russian outside the garage and the cars start up. Both Jack and I put on tight leather gloves.

The elevator starts to rumble. I put my shoulder to the shed door.

As the garage entrance door opens, the swell of organ music fills the room momentarily and then returns to a hush as the door slams shut. Shoes shuffle against the cement, a man grunts, and what has to be the casket scrapes into the hearse.

I smoothly sweep open the door and scamper around the side of the hearse, my left hand loosely holding a worn leather sap. The first man is securing the casket. Dressed in black slacks and a matching blazer with a driver's cap, he doesn't even look up. I slam down the sap into the back of his skull and he slumps to the cement with a quiet groan.

In my peripheral vision, I see Jack slide out of the shed and scramble behind the hood, kneeling to avoid detection. I take three quick strides toward the other man, sap raised. He utters a small shriek just as I strike and raises his arm in defense.

The sap glances off his wrist and smashes into his clavicle. He shrieks again, louder this time, and falls to the floor. I ride him down, savagely swinging the sap. The third blow smashes into his temple and he finally goes limp.

Cursing softly, I drag him toward the shed.

"Hurry," I pant at Jack. "Get the other guy."

I roll my man into the shed as Jack drags the other one over. He rapidly wraps them both in liberal amounts of duct tape and shuts the shed door.

Jack brushes himself off and dons the driver's cap as I tug the casket halfway from the hearse. I take a breath and swing open the casket. The corpse's eyes stare at me. I think I recognize him as the guard who made me lift up my skirt.

Shuddering, I clamber into the casket. I lay down on the corpse, and it's like cold cement. The corpse's head lolls and its mouth clacks open, as if preparing to bite me. I cross the two Uzis against my chest and settle myself.

"Close it," I say to Jack, who stands over me with a horrified expression.

I hear Russian voices right outside.

"Don't talk to anyone," I say. "Just drive out and follow the escort."

"See you on the other side," Jack says. He slams down the casket lid, slides it back on the rollers, and shuts the door.

I feel him inch the big car forward. Through the casket, I can hear surprisingly well.

"Come on, come on…" Jack says to himself.

Someone knocks on the window, his heavy ring sharp against the glass. I hear the door latch tried and failed. Locked. More raps on the window again, clearly angry.

I hear Jack fumble with the window controls for a moment, but he eventually figures out to lower it. "Yes?"

The man snaps something at him in Russian.

"What?" Jack asks.

Somebody large gets in and the hearse settles even lower on its wheels.

The man grumbles some Russian at Jack, who has no way to answer. I begin to panic but then I hear a yell from outside.

"Ready?"

"*Da!*" the man yells and Jack clunks the hearse into gear.

On the highway, the car is silent until the car phone chirps. The Russian answers with a gruff voice. "*Da?* You have word. Zhukov always honor deal. We wait on you."

No idea what any of it means.

Twenty minutes later, the hearse stops. The casket and I are pulled out a few moments later. I'm worried that they'll detect my additional weight, but they lift the casket without complaint.

They march to the grave, singing in a low voice what sounds like a Russian hymn. I wonder who might come to my own funeral. Victor and Cora, of course, and maybe Jack if he wasn't already dead himself.

I feel the casket lowered and deposited. A moment later I hear a voice.

"*V uverennoy i opredelennoy nadezhde na voskreseniye k vechnoy zhizni cherez Gospoda nashego Iisusa Khrista,*" intones what must be the rabbi. "*My otsenivayem Vsemogushchemu Bogu, nash brat Dmitriya.*"

I take a deep breath.

"*Pust' lyubov' seychas napravlyat' Dmitriya.*"

I push open the lid. Blood-red rose petals slide from the casket and flutter around me as I stand up with both Uzis extended.

But I can't see anything. The glare of the sun is too much for my eyes that have adjusted to the darkness of the casket. Damn it. Just another stupid detail that gets people killed. In this case, probably me.

I wipe my eyes with one forearm, swivel, and try to pick up a target. I can barely see the rabbi in his dark suit, who moans and drops his prayer book. It falls to the ground with a heavy thud.

I see Zhukov finally, but he is surrounded by several women and even some kids in blue suits. Two men fling him to the ground and jump on top of him.

My indecision ends when two men draw pistols from their coats.

In the distance I hear the hearse's engine start just as my Uzis spit lead with a sharp *cak-cak-cak*. The two men holding pistols fall back into the crowd. I spray bullets into some men who rush me. Gunshots come from my left and bullets splinter the casket. I roll backward, landing heavily on a marble headstone but manage to sprawl sidewise behind it. Bright white puffs of powdered marble mark the shots as the Russians fire at me.

This is not going well.

The hearse careens toward me. It fishtails into a headstone and sucks it under the car. The wheels spit gravel and the engine revs heavily as the tires struggle to gather traction in the loose dirt and grass.

The Russians ignore their fallen comrades and race out to flank me. I cut down several men. I see Jack's face behind the windshield frozen like a snapshot, pinched in intense concentration, his mouth clamped shut and his eyes blazing. One rose petal somehow drifts across my vision in the wind.

The tires finally catch and Jack hurtles toward me. I roll around the headstone, flinching as bullets snap past. Men, women, and children are shrieking. Jack runs over two men as the hearse gets closer. One gargles a scream while the other just disappears under the wheels with a wet crunch. Shots begin to tear into the hearse. The windows on the passenger side shatter.

I spray the men again and face the hearse as it bears down on me. Men scatter. Jack applies the brakes slightly and I hook an arm through an open window and whip myself into the back. Jack floors it, the tires chirping as we contact the asphalt driveway. He glances back into the casket compartment at me. "You hit?"

I shake my head.

Jack races through the cemetery gate and up the street. After a few blocks, we pull up to the sedan we had stashed earlier. Sirens began to wail in the distance. I slide into the driver's seat, jam the keys into the ignition, and start the car. I force myself to ease away at the speed limit.

A few minutes later, coasting along in interstate traffic, Jack begins to shake. His teeth chatter and sweat pours from his body. He vomits on the floorboard.

"It's the adrenaline," I say.

He retches again. "So stupid," he moans. "Told you that plan was crazy. Did you at least kill Zhukov?"

"No, but we tried. Roland would have appreciated the gesture."

Jack just shakes his head. "Crazy."

May 19, 1973, 5:56 P.M.

"I'll be sad when you're dead."

Pablo fills a bucket with dirty water and hands it to me. "Remember, watch for me to identify the person, and be very apologetic."

Small bugs and sticks float in the bucket, and rainbows from old motor oil bounce on the surface. I hoist the bucket to my waist, one hand on the handle, one on the bottom. I stand on a stone and wood bridge that spans a narrow street built into the slopes of a hill. On the outskirts of Cartagena, the buildings sag against each other like rows of crooked decaying teeth.

"I'll be ready," I say. "Pour and apologize."

"I've never heard you apologize," Pablo says, his eyes squinted with what I think is amusement. "Let's hear it."

"I'm sorry."

Pablo laughs. "You need practice. Something like, 'Oh, I'm so sorry, I slipped and I've ruined everything, how can you ever forgive me?'"

"I'll say whatever you want."

Pablo snorts. "Whatever you do, you need to distract

them. Keep their attention on you no matter what." He puts on his hat and straightens his suit. "Watch for my signal."

I watch him march down the stairs and station himself up the street. He slouches in the shadow of an alley, his face hidden by the brim of his hat.

I watch people hurry along the street. Some look rich, some poor. I pay special attention to the women, looking for my mother. I worry she won't recognize me with my short hair. Almost too late, I see Pablo waving one hand, trying to get my attention. After so long waiting, I'm surprised and freeze for just a moment. He jabs his hand again at a young man in black slacks and a big-collared shirt. I come to my senses and grab the bucket. As he walks below me, I pour it directly on him.

The water splashes on one shoulder and onto his shoes, spattering the stone walkway and bringing him to a stop with a stream of curses. He looks up and sees me holding the bucket. "Look what you've done!" he bellows.

"I'm so sorry, sir, the bucket slipped," I call down.

Pablo runs up to the soaked man. "Oh, that's horrible. Let me help." Pablo starts patting the man with his hand, clucking as he tries to dry him off.

"I'm going to have you arrested!" the man shouts up at me.

"I'm very sorry, dear sir," I yell back. "Please accept my apologies!"

"*Tú me estás jodiendo!*" yells the man, hands reaching up toward me as if he could strangle me. I take a step back, dragging the bucket with me. He looks very angry. Even Pablo looks outraged at my carelessness.

"You stay right there," Pablo shouts. "You're going to pay for this." He sprints under the bridge, toward a staircase that leads away from where I'm standing. That's my signal to run the other way across the bridge and meet him at our rendezvous.

The empty bucket banging against my hip, I dart through several twisting alleys until it would be nearly impossible to guess which way I went. I like the way the switchblade feels as it bounces around in my boot as I run. Breathless and grinning, I arrive at the courtyard at the same time as Pablo. He holds up a wallet and a watch. "Success! Despite your poor apologies!"

I examine the watch. It looks to my eyes like it has been stolen from an emperor. The glass face sparkles and the watch hands glitter. "It must be priceless," I whisper.

"It isn't a good watch," Pablo says, "but we can sell it for something." He opens the wallet and pulls out a small wad of bills, more money than I've seen in my entire life. "He looked like a waiter coming off his shift. They always have cash." Pablo throws the wallet in the gutter. "Ready? We have more work to do. Follow me, I know another good place."

Pablo walks ahead, looking like a wealthy son of some merchant or perhaps a tourist. I trudge fifteen paces behind him with my head down, just another laborer on his way to some ditch.

We perch on a ledge that overlooks a wide sidewalk leading to a piazza. "This time cover your mouth with you hand. Try to look horrified, apologize like you really mean it."

"But my mouth will be covered," I say, trying not to smile.

Pablo sighs. "You can take your hand away while you're talking. It's like a theater show."

"What's a theater show?" I say, still kidding but just barely. I had never been to a theater or movie or anything like that.

Pablo closes his eyes in exasperation. "Never mind. Just try to look sorrier."

He positions himself on the sidewalk below, leaning against a brick wall. A blackened crack zigzags through the crumbling mortar. I gaze down the street, examining each woman's face to see if it matches my memory of my mother. Some are too old, some too young. What will she say if we meet? Will she explain why she left? Why she made Papa and me so sad?

Pablo points to a woman in a linen suit holding a purse. She reminds me of Amelia, her face broad and friendly. Far too nice for a bath of dirty water, I decide, and shake my head. He points again and I shrug. Shaking his head in disgust and anger, he leans back against the wall and we both look up the street.

I see Reuben a moment later and I turn to stone. The *narco* walks slowly along the sidewalk, the sun gleaming off his new boots. I remember the sour smell of him, his foul breath. He swaggers down the street, the same camera hanging from a leather strap around his neck. He smiles at a group of schoolgirls and holds out his camera, wanting them to pose. They giggle and shake their heads. My heart thuds against my chest, and I wonder if I'm dying. The bucket slips from my fingers and I distantly feel the water soak into my boots. I squeeze my eyes tight but my tears burn through anyway, sliding down my nose to drip into the dirt.

The switchblade nestled in my boot chafes against my ankle as I wobble away, looking for a place to hide. The doors to the crooked houses and shacks are all closed; there's nowhere to go if Reuben chooses to climb the stairs. The fear has squeezed my lungs so tight that I can barely breathe.

I edge along the path, pressed against the wooden fence fronting a small house built into the cliffs. The peeling paint flakes off as I slide along the dirty slats. Its cellar offers a place out of sight, but I'm stopped by the faded skull-and-bones symbol tacked onto the entrance. Sudden memories of hiding from Reuben in the poison hut flood into me.

I hear footsteps behind me. There is no time to hide, nowhere to go. I see Reuben on me, his mouth on me, his men throwing me into the back of the truck like a sack of trash. I remember the look on my father's face when Reuben visited us on the beach. A flash of white anger steadies me, and I slip my hand into my boot and pull out the switchblade. The blade flashes from the handle as hot and fast as the anger that gives me life.

It's Pablo, breathing hard. The smile on his face slides off when he sees me, and he takes a step back. "*Qué chingados es eso?*" He puts up his hand. "What's wrong? I looked up and you were gone."

I swallow and take a breath, then drop the knife back into the boot. "Nothing."

"Where did you get the knife?"

"None of your business."

Pablo nods, his lips pursed in a small pucker, and gazes at me with a mixture of annoyance and concern. "You've been crying, you spilled your bucket, and then you pull a knife on me. I think it's time to go home. You're a shitty helper." With that he walks away.

I pick up the bucket, wipe my eyes, and follow. I only care about killing Reuben now. I relish the anger. So much better than what I had before.

After a while, Pablo slows and I catch up. When we reach

the edge of the town and nobody's around, he stops. "If you're going to carry a knife, you should know how to use it. You will never have strength like a man, so quickness is even more important for you." He pulls from his back pocket his own knife, strangely folded together.

"It's called a butterfly knife. Watch!" He grabs one folded handle and swings it out, then quickly flicks it back, and somehow he has a blade pointing at me.

"How'd you do that?"

"Practice. Doesn't matter. Your knife is different. Flick out your blade, then hold it like a hammer, but upside down," he says, demonstrating. The knife is in his fist, the blade pointing to the ground. "Now just bend your wrist so the blade presses up the side of your arm. See?"

I see the knife pressed against his forearm. I pull my switchblade and mimic him.

"Good," he says. "Now just let your arms hang loose. You are holding a knife, but nobody can tell. Make sure the edge is facing outward. Then when you swing, let it rotate out a little. Slash for the throat. If you cut the throat, you will live and they will die. If they block, you will still slash their hands. Then just reverse and swing back for a stab in their heart or maybe neck."

This is more than I've ever heard Pablo say at one time.

"You will probably still die," he finishes. "But maybe not if you are quick enough."

I think about slashing Reuben's throat until we reach Amelia's tin-sheet house. Pablo bangs on her door and then hands me his hat. "Hold this." He pulls stolen watches, wallets, coins, small purses, and a couple strange bags filled with white crystals from his pockets and drops them into the hat. Then he strips out of his suit, completely heedless of me and Amelia.

"Take your pick and give me back my clothes."

Amelia peers into the hat and after a moment withdraws a small purse. "I washed your trousers and shirt," Amelia says. "They smell much better."

As Pablo dresses, I look into the hat and examine the strange plastic bags filled with a white powder.

"I'm keeping the hat," Pablo says to Amelia, who just nods. He grabs it from me, and we march back the way we came this morning but as we reach the edge of the *favela*, he stops. He sits on the ground and intently unwraps one of the bags of powder and makes a small pile of the white crystal powder on his bent knee. With a jerk, he rams his nostril into the powder and inhales.

I watch in amazement. What is he doing?

Pablo stands back up and wipes his nose. "Don't say anything to Miguel."

I nod. "What is that?"

"It's what the *narcos* make. *Cocaína*. They carry it in their pockets sometimes. That *pendejo* with the camera was a *narco*, so I lifted it from him."

"His name is Reuben."

Pablo looks at me. "Was he one of the guys who took you?"

I don't say anything.

"It's dangerous to steal from the *narcos*," Pablo says. "If they catch you, they'll snort the *cocaína* and blame it on you. A boy named Antonio used to come with me, and he got caught." He licks the *cocaína* off of his fingers. "They killed him, I think." Pablo offers me the other bag of powder. "Do you want to try it? I think you'll like it."

I suddenly know what to do.

"I'll take half. And the bag."

"The bag? Why?"

A little bit of hope mixes with my anger and I grin at Pablo. "I'll tell you later."

"What?" he says, confused.

"I'm going to kill Reuben."

Pablo opens the second bag of *cocaína*. "Leave him alone, Reno. He's better at killing than you." He dips his nose into the bag, pauses, and looks back up at me before he snorts. "Even if you could kill him, you wouldn't get away with it."

"I don't care," I say.

"I'll be sad when you're dead," he says and inhales directly from the bag.

July 29, 1986, 4:37 P.M.

"Cordite, blood, gasoline, smoke, whatever."

I shove a Bible farther down the pew, sit down, and listen to the choir. Their hymn fills the vaulted ceilings. It fills me with a gentle spirit, but after a while my curiosity compels me to my feet. I drift to the side of the confessional and press my ear against it.

Father Ramirez is talking calmly, as if to a child. "You're missing the point, Victor. Whether it is premeditated or accidental, it doesn't matter. You can't make deals with God. He doesn't trade favors, and He doesn't tally points."

"Look, Father, I'm trying to leave my old life behind me. But in order for that to happen, I have to take certain steps."

"The police visited here earlier," Father Ramirez says quietly. "Asking about you. Do you think they agree with your philosophy?"

"What did you tell them?"

"Why do you need to know?"

"Just tell me."

"Or what? Will you silence me as well?"

"It's not like that," Victor sighs. "Why do you have to

make everything so hard? Please, just tell me what you told them."

"I told them nothing," Father Ramirez says icily. "But I had hoped you would follow Christ's example, Victor. Violence is not the answer."

"It might not be the answer but it's often the perfect solution. You can ask Maria about how well Christ's teachings convinced her pimp to release her."

Silence.

"I know the Russians are going to retaliate, and I'm not prepared. My security staff is very small, and most are inexperienced. Losing Roland just makes it worse."

"Roland died?"

"Yeah."

"I'm so sorry. How many others?"

"That died? Many. I wish more had died, Father. I wish they had all died."

"Victor—"

Victor's voice rises. "You want to help, Father? Say a prayer for an old friend. His name was Gartello. See if that will bring him back. While you're at it, buy yourself a fucking lottery ticket."

The confessional door bangs open like a shot. I whirl away but not in time. Victor stares at me from the doorframe. "What are you doing?"

"Nothing. Just listening to the choir."

"The choir?"

"Yeah. It's pretty."

"We're going. Carter wants to meet."

I wonder what Father Ramirez thinks after we leave. Does he say a prayer? Mutter a curse? Probably both, I think as I push the sedan through traffic toward Carter's decrepit warehouse. Victor is right. The Russians are not going to forget what I did at the funeral.

Abandoned cars and graffiti-covered trucks clutter the curb along Carter's block. I reluctantly park halfway up the street.

"If anything feels bad for any reason, you just stop and turn around," I say to Victor. "Don't run, just turn around and walk back to the car. I'll take it from there." I roll down the window and stick my head out into the breeze.

"What are you doing?"

"Smelling."

"For what?"

"Cordite, blood, gasoline, smoke, whatever."

Victor raises his eyebrows. "Cordite?"

"Smell goes straight to the brain. There's a chance a smell would trigger a response before any of my other senses could register. I wouldn't be surprised if Zhukov blew up an entire block to get us."

"Let me out," he says.

I exit the sedan and open Victor's door just as I see Jack pull open the front door of Carter's warehouse. He brushes past someone in a hooded sweatshirt, who steps onto the street and hurriedly walks away. Something tickles at me… Where have I seen him before?

A few moments later, I rap on Carter's door. It jerks open and Carter waves us inside. Jack hugs me, and my day brightens.

"I just got back from processing the graveyard," Carter says. "Dead Russians everywhere you look. Run over. Shot. Shot and run over. It's like, well, a fucking graveyard."

Victor eyes Carter's living room with disdain, taking in the specimen jars. The parrot flaps under the black felt tarp covering his cage. "What did you want to talk about?" he asks Carter.

Carter sucks his teeth. "We got a problem."

"What now?" Victor asks tiredly.

Carter pushes out his lips in a pucker. He raises his flat palms and lowers them with a sigh. "The same damn problem as before. We need to talk about Carmen. I got her into the safe house like you wanted, but she won't wait long. We need to get her out now."

"She'll wait," Jack says.

"Oh, yeah? Look at this. Hot off the presses." Carter inserts a tape into his VCR.

I see Carmen sitting glumly at a kitchen table, handcuffed to a stainless ring bolted to the tabletop.

"Hey, it's about time," she says as Larry sits down across from her. "I ain't heard from you in two days, and I'm beginning to think you're full of shit."

Larry nods slowly. "That's ironic. I was just thinking the same about you."

Carmen sits quietly, eyes on the table. Finally she looks up at him. "We already had this conversation. You know the deal—just get the DA to agree and I'll come through on my end."

"Yeah, that's right. We had that conversation, and that was the deal. But I think we need a different deal."

"Look, I really have no idea where you're going with this."

"I'm done playing games with you," he says evenly. "You're going to tell me everything you know right now."

Carmen cocks her head and looks at him like she used to look at me. I can see that Larry doesn't like it any more than I did. "No, I'm not. Not without the deal on the table," she says, the disdain in her voice making her even less likeable.

"How about I just walk you back to the hole? Maybe you can cut another deal in there. See what you can give the Russians in return for a shank to your liver. I don't need you that badly, Carmen."

Carmen purses her lips. "Okay, fine. You bring the DA or anyone else you want tomorrow, and I'll tell you enough to wipe out half your department and Pagnolli at the same time."

Carter stops the tape. "Just like I told you. She isn't going to wait."

"You arrested her," Victor says. "Now you can't cut a deal, and your partner is making it worse."

That familiar feeling of dread fills my veins, and it feels like gravity is crushing me. "There has to be some way to change her mind," I say.

"In fact, there is a way," Carter replies. "I had a word with our friend Carmen afterward. She'll walk if I can get her out tomorrow."

"So get her out," Jack says.

Carter shakes his head. "My plan involves some coordination and trust, and Carmen doesn't trust me."

"Shocker," I say.

"But she'll agree to keep her mouth shut if we can get her some money and some leverage." Carter cocks his hand into the shape of a gun and points it at me. "My gun. No need for trust then."

"She wants your gun?" I ask.

"Are you fucking deaf?" Carter takes a hit from his inhaler and glares at me. "Yes, she wants my gun. So she'll have some leverage."

"How does she even know we have your gun?" I ask. "What the hell is going on here?" I say.

Carter shrugs. "Ask loverboy."

I look at Jack, who holds up a hand. "I told her."

"Why would you tell her *that*?" I yell.

"I needed to convince her that she wasn't getting set up. I thought if she knew we had Carter's gun, she'd trust that we had him under control. I didn't expect her to ask for it. She's really angry with me, and doesn't trust me anymore, I had to offer her something."

"What else did you say to her? And what else haven't you told us?"

Jack's lips press together into a thin line. "That's why I came over—to hash this out, let you know the deal."

Victor shakes his head. "Difficult for me to trust that Carter will give the pistol to Carmen."

Carter puts his fingertips on his temples and pushes the words from his lips one at a time. "Yes, I know that. You don't trust me, Carmen doesn't trust me, Reno doesn't trust me. Nobody trusts me. You don't have to keep saying it." He closes his eyes for a moment. "And Carmen doesn't trust Jack any more either." He shoots a glance at me. "In fact, she hates him. If he wants to fuck Reno's panties off, hey, I get that, but Carmen somehow doesn't share my appreciation."

"Go fuck yourself," I say.

"Duly noted. But point of fact, I have no money, no gun, and frankly, you can go fuck yourself too, Reno. I'm trying to help. You're just being a bitch."

"Let's kill her," I say.

"I told you we weren't doing that," Jack says.

Carter looks morose. Not that I care about him or his fucking problems, but for once we actually did have a shared interest. I wonder if Carmen really would just disappear or whether she'd keep fucking up my life.

"She gets the gun, she drops off the face of the earth," Victor says. He points a finger at Jack. "You tell her that."

"Carmen isn't too excited about seeing Jack," Carter says. "I'll do it."

"No. You and Reno will do it together."

"I have the night shift," Carter says. "I'll relieve Larry, disable the video feed for a minute, and then some bad people must have followed me because I get knocked out and when I wake up, Carmen is gone. Simple." He shrugs. "But like I said, Carmen won't do it without the gun. She doesn't trust me. She was emphatic on that point."

"Smart girl," I say.

July 29, 1986, 10:17 P.M.

"We have switchblade for heart."

"I don't need a babysitter," I say to Jack.

"I know, I know. I'm just a little insurance policy in case something goes wrong." He hands me Carter's service revolver. "But everything should go fine. I'll just follow Carter in case of emergencies."

"Yeah, okay," I say.

A moment later Carter rolls into the Last Call parking lot in his dented Cadillac. Another ride with Carter. I take one last look at my Ducatti parked across the street, think maybe I should just follow Carter.

"Come on!" he yells at me.

"We okay?" asks Jack.

"Let's talk after," I say. Maybe with Carmen out of our lives we can find a good path together. I hope so.

I slide into the Cadillac. Carter's bloated pale face winces as if in pain, but I see him try to shape his wrecked grimace into smile through his swollen red lips. It is like watching a diseased clown give birth to an aneurism.

"You don't look too good," I say.

"Neither do you."

"I look better than you."

"Got the gun?"

"Arrangements have been made."

"What the hell does that mean? You either have it or you don't."

"Not your problem."

Carter moodily stares out the window as he eases through the late-night traffic, each glaring headlight stabbing my eyes and deepening my headache.

"This'll just take a second," Carter says. He pulls into the parking lot of a liquor store.

"What are we doing here?"

"Always prepare for victory."

A couple of kids, probably no more than eleven or twelve, stand nervously near the door. They stare at us as we step out of the sedan. For a wild moment, I think they're robbing the store, but I relax when they slouch out of our way.

Carter glides over to the chilled cases and pulls out a bottle of vodka. "I like how the cold makes my throat ache," he says.

I just shake my head and wish that Roland were still alive.

The two kids walk toward us. They look like they're brothers.

"Kind of late for you, isn't it?" Carter says to the youngest one. "It's way past your bedtime, partner."

The older one reaches into a basket near the counter and removes a miniature bottle of rum, his small fist swallowing the even smaller bottle. He mutely holds it out to Carter.

"What? You want me to buy that for you?"

Both of them nod.

"Are you shitting me?" He looks at the clerk, who just

shrugs. Carter snorts. "You little idiots. You shoplift these, you don't pay for them."

"Hey!" the clerk objects.

"And besides, stay away from rum and scotch. That shit will kill you. Stick to vodka." He shakes his bottle of Stolichnaya at them.

"Please…" says the older kid. He shoves the tiny bottle into Carter's blotchy hand. "It's only a buck."

Carter shrugs and puts the bottle on the counter. "Don't say I didn't warn you." He pays the clerk, who is looking more and more perturbed. Carter tosses the oldest one the tiny bottle. "Look, you're better off skipping booze altogether. Crack's your ticket. Just go down two blocks and suck some guy off for a few rocks. It'll turn your whole life around."

The clerk shoves the vodka at Carter. "Get out. You're not helping."

"Hey, at least I don't sell this shit for a living," Carter sneers. "Fucking hypocrite."

"Okay, get out, all of you. I'm calling the cops."

Carter pauses, and I can tell he wants to pull his badge, but in a show of amazing judgment for him, he marches to the sedan and we're off again. Carter takes long pulls from the vodka bottle as he drives.

When we merge onto the highway, Carter slouches down in his seat and turns off the headlights. The highway becomes a smooth black ribbon. Carter rolls down the windows, and the wind roars through the sedan.

"For the first time today I don't feel like dying!" he yells at me over the wind. He is swallowing vodka and smiling, and the wind pushes tears from his eyes and down his cheeks. He laughs wildly as we rocket through the darkness, the brake lights of cars in front of us smearing the windshield.

I just sit there wishing he was dead. I hope Jack can keep up. I hadn't seen him following us, but he said he would keep out of sight.

Fortunately, we reach our exit just a few minutes later. Carter turns the lights back on and cruises his Cadillac down the streets until we're about a block away from the safe house.

"Wait until Larry leaves, then quickly come around back," Carter instructs me. He points out a two-story brick house. Several alleys run adjacent to it—should be easy to get in or out.

I let my eyes adjust to the darkness as I get the feel of the neighborhood. It looks blue collar, run down but quiet. It won't pick up until people start getting up for the early shift. I mentally note any open windows or dogs or anything that could betray our presence. This block is pretty industrial, which is good. Probably no pets and maybe not a lot of tenants, if we're lucky. But I haven't felt lucky in a long time.

"Anyone else in the house?"

"No, just Larry and Carmen. Give me a minute."

I get out of the car and stand in the shadow of a rusted bus stop littered with cigarette butts. Carter pulls the Cadillac up to the house and enters. A few minutes later, I see Larry climb into a gold Oldsmobile and drive away.

I look for Jack, but there's no sign of him.

I make my way down the side of the house and squat in the darkness near the back door. Just as he'd promised, Carter opens up the back door a few minutes later and I enter the kitchen. The look on Carmen's face is priceless. Stark terror.

"Don't hurt me, please," Carmen says. Her right hand is cuffed to the steel ring bolted to the kitchen table.

"You still don't get it, do you?" Carter takes a hit off his inhaler. "We're here to break you out, you stupid sack of shit."

An angry frown slashes her face. "Yeah, sure. You and Reno, huh?"

He shakes his head, exasperated. "Don't piss me off. It can still go the other way if you push me far enough." He shakes out a key. "Help me out here," he says to me. "Hold on to her so she doesn't bolt."

I get behind the table and grab Carmen from behind. "Relax," I say.

"Carter was supposed to bring the gun, not you."

"It's all going to work out," I say.

Carter unlocks Carmen from the handcuff. With a lightning-quick twist she grabs my arm and before I can react, Carter slaps the steel cuff around my wrist. I pull away, but Carmen is clawing at me and Carter pushes me down on the table. Another cuff loops around my other wrist.

The laughter from Carter bursts out in a deranged howl.

I jerk the cuffs against the table. "Very funny. Take this off."

Carmen and Carter dance around the living room, laughing.

Panting slightly with tears rolling down his veiny cheeks, Carter laughs. "So perfect!"

"Take the cuffs off, you asshole. This is no time to fuck around," I say in the most bored, casual way possible but my mouth is suddenly bone dry.

To my relief, he approaches with a smile and shakes out his key again. "Come on, I'm just kidding."

But then he slugs me in the mouth with a short brutal punch. My vision dims. I vaguely see his arm piston back. I hear a noise like a melon hit by a bat and the world spins. Blood runs down my throat. I distantly feel his hands roughly run up and down my body until he finds his gun and pulls it from my jacket.

I look up after what seems like a while and Carter hits me again, splitting my lips.

Panting, Carter leers at me. "You fucking bitch, how do you like it?"

The initial shock of the situation begins to fade, replaced with a hot anger. The look of gloating on Carter's face drives a spike of fury into my brain. I gather a mouthful of blood and phlegm and spit it into Carter's face.

"MOTHERFUCKER!" he screams. He wipes his face and looks at me with such a hate that fear shoots through my body.

I hear the back door open and shut.

Steps approach. Jack?

Carter and Carmen turn their heads as Zhukov and Golnak enter the kitchen.

"Just like I told you," Carter gloats. "She's practically wrapped in a bow."

"You'll die for this, Carter," I slur, my lips swollen and bloody.

Zhukov holds up a hand before Carter can hit me again. "Tsk, tsk, Reno. That is not good way to start. Carter tries to, how you say, simply grow his career. Your capitalism allows marketplace to determine value of him. And to the highest bidder he goes, yes?"

"You're all going to die," I say.

Zhukov scratches his ear. "Eventually." He squats on his heels and peers at me. "Reno, I am not subtle person. Neither are you. We try in past to kill each other." He shrugs. "So you probably think now I kill you."

"You'll kill me just like you killed Gartello," I say bleakly. "The same man who helped you and treated you with more respect than you deserved."

"I not kill Gartello for fun. I like him. But you and Victor are pets to him. He spoil you." He shrugs again. "He will not resolve things like he promise. You rob me and kill my men. You disrupt a funeral, make my children cry, so I must do the things that he will not." Zhukov regards me for a moment. "Every day people walk by me. Most of them good. They open door, they say hello, smile, maybe help change punctured tire, *da*? But the law of averages always must apply. If some are saints, some must be sinners, yes?" He smiles. "That is you and me. We have switchblade for heart."

I focus on breathing.

"Because you are worthy enemy, Reno, I wanted to say good-bye in person. I was hoping to see Victor too, but perhaps another time. *Spokojnoj nochi.*"

"*Pozvol'te mne ubit' yeye,*" Golnak says.

"*Nyet, ya obeshchal yey Carter. Eto bylo soglasheniye.*"

Golnak bitterly shakes his head.

"He asks to kill you himself," Zhukov says to me. "But that will serve no good purpose. I promised you to Carter, and you know I never tell lie."

May 22, 1973, 12:45 P.M.

"But still *magnified*"

We leave Amelia's the same way as before, but this time Pablo is wearing dark blue trousers and a white cotton shirt that's already speckled with sweat. He has a small book bag slung over his shoulders. Clumps of students are common on the streets during lunch, and he'll fit right in.

"Just like last time," he says as we walk. "Try to actually look sorry. Distract them a little while I yell at you and help dry them off."

"I'll be very sorry," I lie.

"Sorrier than last time. And don't do anything stupid with the *narcos*. Let me handle it. You just bump them."

"Whatever you say," I lie again. My hand creeps into my pocket and I squeeze the bag of my own *cocaína*, thinking of Reuben and his camera. Maybe I'll take a picture of *him* this time. See how he likes it.

An hour later we're stationed on a street that Pablo says makes him feel lucky. I'm hoping that luck will rub off on me as I balance my bucket of dirty water on a cracked wooden rail that lines a worn staircase leading up to a cluster of equally decrepit houses dug into the hillside. An old woman peers at me from a window, the glass missing, curtain ruffling in the coastal breeze. I smile at her but she stares back at me stonily.

I refuse to dump water on an old man who looks kind, much to Pablo's frustration, and then I also refuse to help him pickpocket a woman who reminds me of my mother. He glares at me, and I shrug. But eventually I do consent to dump a bucket of dirty water on an unsuspecting and probably equally innocent pedestrian and apologize frantically while Pablo robs him.

But the man's wallet turns out to be completely empty. "*Este hombre era sabio!*" Pablo says admiringly as he shakes the wallet in frustration. "He must have had two. He fooled me. Asshole."

We relieve the next man of a small bundle of blue marbles, which actually pleases Pablo. "Miguel will let me keep these."

In the afternoon we migrate to the same street where we saw Reuben, and I know Pablo is looking for *narcos*. I say a small prayer for nothing more than fairness, afraid to pray for revenge. My life for Reuben's. That seems fair.

My bucket is empty. Pouring water like last time will only alert them to pickpockets. The plan is for me to jostle and bump our marks and let Pablo's quick hands dip into their pockets while they are distracted by me.

Pablo slouches against a pillar, lazily digging in his bag for something. Just another soft student looking for his lost homework or a late afternoon snack. But I can see his eyes dart up the street, casting for targets.

Hours go by, and as the shadows darken the cobblestones I start thinking that maybe today is not the day. But then I see him and another man saunter down the street. His boots gleam even in the dusk. Pablo straightens, slings his book bag over his shoulder, and begins to slowly walk toward them, kicking pebbles as he goes.

I check for my bag of *cocaína* and clump down the stairs, my big boots bouncing on the dirt path that leads to the main street. I keep my head down, peeking at Reuben from under the battered *quinciano* covering my face. He's walking ahead of me, the crowd recognizing a *narco* and giving him plenty of room. I sense Pablo behind me, but I don't care. It'll be easier to get caught if he doesn't interfere. Reuben nears a curve in the street by a sewer grate and I know this is my chance.

I walk straight up to Reuben and dip into his jacket pocket as I bump him hard. Nothing, just the empty silk lining. He spins toward me as I dip his other pocket. My desperate fingers find the small bundle, and I purposely trip just as one of his hands grabs me.

"*¿Que coño?*" he yells, grabbing my wrist. "Got you, *pendejo!*" We both fall to the ground, and I flick his small bag of *cocaína* into the sewer grate while my other hand holds my bag. I struggle to pull away from him, but he finds his balance and pulls himself back onto his feet, with me dangling on my tiptoes in his grip.

Reuben punches me square in the forehead. Stars burst around me and I stagger. He pulls at my fist, trying to pry it open. I resist with all my strength but there's no stopping him. "*¡Cuca!*" he says when he finally bends back my fingers and sees my packet of *cocaína*. "You are a thief, a very stupid and idiotic thief!" He pulls my face to his. "Do you know what happens to people who steal from us?"

He slaps me, and more stars appear. My hat falls off, but he doesn't seem to recognize me. "Bring him along, Cacho. I want Esteban to hear about this."

Reuben pockets my *cocaína*, and I protest and cry as Cacho, smelling of stale sweat and tobacco, roughly drags me along.

We only get a block away before Pablo appears in front of us. "Leave him alone," he says, his eyes squinted into slits.

Reuben and Cacho come to a stop.

"Stay away, Pablo," I yell at him. "Run!"

Reuben laughs. "Best advice you'll get today. Your friend stole from me, and that can't be tolerated."

"He's my brother. I'll have our father beat him for you. Let him go."

Reuben snorts, and Cacho starts to drag me along again, heading right for Pablo.

"I'll be okay!" I yell at Pablo. "Just go home." This isn't part of my plan. I never imagined that Pablo would try to save me. I expected him to run, not fight.

Pablo's arms are slack at his sides, and I know he's drawn his hidden knife.

"Your father has two stupid kids," Reuben says. "But not for long."

Pablo pivots on one foot and lashes out his arm. I see the blade flash toward Reuben's throat. Either Reuben knows the trick or his reactions are superb. He arches his back like a snake, his camera slinging around his neck by its tethers, as Pablo's knife whips by.

Reuben lets himself fall backward, not trying to catch his balance, but scissor-kicks his legs. His boot catches Pablo's jaw, spinning him around to the ground with a *thump*.

Cacho jerks me forward. I bite him in the arm, but he manages to lunge forward and kick Pablo in the gut anyway. Then Cacho hooks a fist into my ear, and I black out.

I awake and open my eyes to the same room where Reuben had wrapped his belt around my head. Cacho's sitting on the ancient, bloodstained gold sofa, examining my bite marks on his arm. Water drips onto me from the rusty corrugated panels above.

Behind me I hear the familiar whirr of Reuben's special camera. I twist my head and see him taking pictures of Pablo.

"Tell your brother to smile," he says. "It might put Esteban in a good mood."

Pablo stares at the floor.

"Your choice," Reuben says. "Here's a present for you," he says to me and throws a picture of Pablo at me. He walks over, sits on the couch next to Cacho, and pulls out the small bundle of *cocaína*. White crystals spill onto the back of his hand.

Reuben smiles at me. "You want some?"

For one horrible moment, I think I'll be forced to inhale his drugs, but then the exit door bangs open. Reuben places one hand over the *cocaína* and casually looks at two men who stand in the entrance. One is loosely carrying a shotgun in one hand. His eyes sweep over Pablo and me like a hawk might regard sparrows. The other man is skinny, wearing a *llanero* shirt buttoned to his neck.

"*Héctor le verán en diez minutos,*" the skinny man says and then slams the door.

I watch Reuben intently. As Cacho stands, Reuben gets up too, and I clench my fists in frustration and anger. All of this for nothing. My switchblade still sits deep in my boot, and I wonder if I could somehow get a blade into his heart.

But then Reuben sits back down. "This won't take long."

I keep my head down, but watch intently from under my brows as my heart thuds in my head.

Reuben opens the packet of *cocaína* he took from me and snorts right from the packet, then jerks his head up. Wipes his nose. "Cacho, this batch is off." He dips his nose into the packet and finishes it. "Definitely off." He shakes his head. "Bitter. But still *magnífico*!" He takes pictures of himself with his camera. "Grab them both," he says to Cacho as he stands.

"If you bite me again, you little asshole, I'll kick out all your teeth," Cacho snarls at me. "Understand?"

I nod with my head down. I stuff the picture of Pablo into my pocket as Cacho pulls me to my feet. Cacho grabs Pablo too, who glances at me. The fear in his face makes me feel sick with guilt. It wasn't supposed to be this way. I assumed he would run. I would have run.

With Cacho herding us from behind, we follow Reuben across a courtyard and into a warehouse, the roof held in place by steel beams rising twenty feet in the air. Men with shotguns stand at each door, the barrels gleaming blue and black. Barrels labeled ACETONE clutter the space, but before I can make out more we are pushed through another door and down a narrow corridor. More men holding shotguns stand at the next door. Their eyes flick back and forth between us, and they nod at Reuben as he approaches.

Reuben pauses for just a moment in front of the closed door. He tucks in his shirt and runs his fingers through his hair. He looks back at Cacho. "¿*Listo*?"

"*Sí.*"

Reuben opens the door, which leads into a large office. Oil paintings of topless women hang on one wall. My boots sink into a lush burgundy carpet. A fat *gringo* sits on a couch opposite the paintings, in the middle of a conversation with tall, skinny hawk-faced man wearing just a leather vest and shiny white slacks.

"Esteban, we have caught more thieves," Reuben announces.

Esteban holds up one finger. "Just a moment." He presses his hands together under his chin like he's about to pray. "Our product is the most pure, but high quality comes at a price," he says to the fat *gringo*. "There are technical challenges making *cocaína* in this country and many costs—bribery, security, and of course I have all kinds of labor problems," he finishes with a look at Reuben.

Reuben starts to speak, but instead his teeth clack down and his head spasms for a moment. He looks confused, but then he gathers himself. "A gang of thieves assaulted us and robbed me, Esteban. They stole the samples and ran, but we caught these two."

"See, Victor?" Esteban says with a smile. "Thieves are everywhere."

"They certainly look ferocious," the man called Victor deadpans. "Your men must fear for their lives."

Esteban frowns. "*Verdad.* Reuben, how you are always getting robbed by children? And where are these two hiding the drugs?"

Reuben twitches again. "They are very fast, picked my pocket, *jefe,* and I think they might have swallowed—" Another spasm jerks his head back. His back arches impossibly backward, and his teeth crunch as his mouth slams shut.

"Reuben?" asks Esteban.

Reuben falls to the floor, and Cacho kneels at his side.

"What is he doing?" Esteban asks with alarm in his voice.

"I don't know, *jefe.*"

The muscles in Reuben's face convulse, pulling his mouth

into a ghastly smile. The skin pulls taut, and I see the bones shine bright from the pressure. His legs shake and a faint tinge of blue begins to form around his eyes. I realize that he can't breathe. A thin shriek comes from deep within him and his fingers flail at his neck. One hand presses the camera button and a milk-white image pushes out.

"Jaime!" Esteban yells. "Get in here!"

The door bursts open and men with shotguns rush in.

One man presses the barrel into Victor's face, another knocks Pablo and me to the floor. Two fall on Reuben, driving knees into his chest and neck.

"No, no, I'm fine," Esteban screams. "We need help for Reuben!"

The men jump off Reuben, who squirms onto his side. Spasms contort him even farther back until his heels are drumming against his skull. The men step back, some making the sign of the cross. Nobody touches him. Reuben's eyes are opened impossibly wide, perhaps about to burst from his skull. He gasps once, and then again.

"*Oh mi Dios de mierda*," one man murmurs.

"Get him out of here," Esteban yelps. "*¡Jesucristo!*"

The men hesitate, but then Cacho grabs Reuben's legs and drags him out of the room. A couple other men awkwardly mill around; one tries to straighten the rug. "Get out!" Esteban yells and finally the door closes.

Pablo's face is white, slack. I am filled with peace. Rat poison and *cocaína* look exactly alike. Stealing rat poison is easy, so is filling an old sample bag. Replacing Reuben's sample bag without him realizing was the hard part, but not too hard for a determined pickpocket who doesn't care if she dies trying.

July 29, 1986, 10:57 P.M.

"Do you want to watch?"

Carter sucks on his inhaler. "I've been waiting for this for a long time," he says, his voice hoarse. "We're going to have some fun together." He steps out of the room and comes back a minute later with some rags, which he starts to knot together into a gag.

A breath of hope. He's not going to kill me immediately, and Jack is still out there. I need to buy some time.

"I'm sorry it went like this, Reno," Carmen says.

"I can't believe you lied to Jack," I say. "You're all liars."

"Honey, this was all Jack's idea," she drawls. "He was just using you to get me free and make good with the Russians."

This latest blow feels like a kick to the stomach. She's lying—she has to be. "Jack wouldn't—"

Carter shoves the gag into my mouth and ties it. I flip Carmen the bird.

"I always admired your spirit, Reno," Carmen says. "I'll give you that much."

"Do you want to watch?" Carter asks her.

Adrenaline jackhammers my heart.

Carmen flinches. "No."

"I'm going to the bathroom," he tells Carmen. "After that I'm going to have some fun. Unless you want to join or watch, you should take off." Carter smiles at me, and then gently cradles my chin. "Don't go anywhere, sweetcheeks, okay?" Then he slams his fist into my ear and the room spins again.

I hear the front door open. I think it's a door. Jack? My imagination? I don't know. I look up and only see Carmen.

"I forgot my—" says a voice. Larry stops in mid-sentence and instantly draws his revolver. The revolver's blue-black barrel sweeps the room, briefly sitting on each of us, then settling on Carmen. "What's going on here, Carmen? Where's Carter?"

Carmen looks at him mutely.

"Face-down on the floor," he yells. "Now!"

I rest my head on the table. Part of me feels a surge of hope and relief. Another part of me just sits dormant, dazed. My head is still ringing from Carter's punches, and one eye won't focus properly. I grunt and tilt my head toward the hallway, trying to warn him about Carter.

"What's going on here, Reno?" Larry says guardedly. "Who hit you? How did you get cuffed?"

I see almost in slow-motion the beautiful cuff key float toward my wrist. Everything is so slow…

"Carter do this to you?" he asks. "What's going on?" He gently removes my gag and I try to talk.

"Yshh…" I say, trying to make my mouth move. As the cuff snaps open, I pull the other cuff through the ring and push away from the table. I stagger to my feet but then I start to spin and fall down onto tile. I can see bits of green lawn grass stuck to Larry's black Oxford shoe.

I take another breath, feel my senses start to collect.

"Carter—" I take another deep breath and try to form the words.

I see a pair of shoes behind Larry and know that there's no more time.

Carter slams the barrel of his gun into Larry's skull with a horrible crunching sound. Larry staggers into the living room, and Carter pounces on him.

I crawl into the side hall leading to the living room as Larry and Carter struggle behind me. Somehow I get to my feet and stumble down the hall, one cuff still attached to my right wrist. It slaps against the wall wildly as I lurch forward. I duck into the first room on the left and hold my breath. I slip my switchblade from my boot and flick open the blade.

Larry moans in the kitchen but the rest of the house is silent.

Bullets whip past my face as Carter fires directly into the wall between us. Streams of light fill the room and a small mirror bordered in roses drops and shatters, scattering winking slivers of glass across the room. Brass shells clatter on the kitchen tile, and the dry smell of dust and drywall fills my nose.

I hear footsteps and then the back door slam. Carmen leaving? Jack? Where the hell is he?

I pick up a large shard of glass from the broken mirror and duck across the hallway into a small bedroom, through a bathroom, and then into another bedroom.

The house is dead silent now.

Carter's gun booms four more times from the adjacent bedroom.

More silence.

I angle my shard of mirror so I can see back up the hallway. Larry groans softly, his eyes open but unseeing. His gun is just sitting there by his knee, but I'd be too exposed if I went for it. Fuck.

"Larry! Larry!" I whisper, trying to get his attention. His eyes rove frantically but they're vacant. No use.

The kitchen looks empty now. Maybe if I jump across Larry, reach him from behind the kitchen wall… I don't like that maneuver at all, but being pinned in this room is even worse.

I gather myself and jump through the hallway gap, just as Larry decides, incredibly, to stand up. I smash into him, sending him back to the floor. I pivot on one foot and spin into the kitchen, off-balance but still holding my knife.

"Stop right there," Carter says, and it feels like my blood has turned to sluggish mud.

Carter levels his gun at me. "I really wanted to play, Reno, but I'll have to do it after you're dead, I guess." He cocks his pistol.

Larry staggers into the kitchen behind Carter, pointing his service revolver at him.

"Don't move," Larry slurs and then stammers out some unintelligible gibberish. He puts one hand on the wall. Blood flows down his neck in a red braid.

Carter's eyes widen. A surge of energy flows through me and I come up on the balls of my feet.

Carter keeps his gun on me, but turns his head to look at Larry. "You don't look too good," he says in a soft voice, as if he was talking to a child. "You got hit on the head. Things got to be a bit fuzzy right now."

Larry closes one eye and shudders. His teeth chatter and for one horrifying moment, I think he's going to fall down. The nozzle of his gun wobbles erratically.

Beads of sweat are blossoming on Carter's brow. His eyes dart between Larry and me. He bends his knees and starts to place his gun on the ground but then he whips the gun around to Larry.

Both Larry and Carter stagger as their guns fire. The simultaneous muzzle flashes dazzle my eyes.

Larry falls backward onto the carpet, his head lolled to the side.

A crimson stain rapidly spreads across Carter's chest. He slumps to his knees and then rolls on his side like a capsizing boat. I tug the gun from his twitching fingers as his voice wheezes out like a ghost calling my name. "Reno…"

I scramble over to Larry and sit him up, feeling for wounds. His leg bleeds profusely and he's trembling with the strain and lost blood. "Keep it together, Larry. You're almost home free," I say as I pull off his tie and wrap it tightly above the wound and double knot it. Blood still pulses from the bullet entry. It's not enough. The dim wail of sirens reaches my ear. I quickly strip a shoelace from his Oxford and cinch it tight enough to stop the bleeding. His white face gapes at me. His mouth moves a little, but no sound escapes his lips.

"Try not to move, Larry! People are coming. Help will be here soon." I put his hand on the laces. "Hold these tight and you'll make it!"

The back door bursts open and footsteps pound down the hallway. I'm too late. I stand up, hands above my head.

It's Jack.

May 22, 1973, 3:09 P.M.

"Everyone is guilty."

"I see what you mean by labor problems," Victor says.

"It's not funny," Esteban snaps. "Stand up!" he yells at Pablo and me. "Did you steal from me?"

I just look at the ground. I knew how it would end, but I feel badly that Pablo will pay the same price as me. He should have run.

"Strip! Off with your clothes!"

We both hesitate, but Esteban starts slapping us and we begin to step out of our dirty boots and pull off our clothes. Soon we are standing in our underwear.

"Oh, what do we have here?" Esteban says. "Not a small boy after all, but a girl. I thought there was something not right with this one."

Esteban sorts through our clothes. He shakes my switchblade from my boot. "So many tricks in this one," he says, flicking the blade out. "So, was Reuben telling the truth? Did you swallow my *cocaína*?" He waves my switchblade in front of us, smiling. "Which one, Victor? Who looks guilty?"

"Everyone is guilty," Victor says. "But they're just kids. Let them go. We have business to finish."

"No, you must pick."

"No."

"Then I will!" Esteban drives my knife into Pablo's gut, viciously yanks upward, and steps back. Blood sprays me as Pablo gasps and drops to the carpet with a tight choking sound. Esteban kicks him, then rips him with the knife again and again. Blood is everywhere, and the world becomes a blur of red as tears fill my eyes. I did this to Pablo.

Finally sated, Esteban rolls Pablo onto his back. I can see his ribs and spine. The knife, my knife, has butchered my friend. Esteban turns to Victor. "No *cocaína* in this one. It must be the girl." He raises the knife and walks toward me.

"Stop," Victor says.

"Everyone is guilty. Isn't that what you say?"

"We have business to finish."

"You don't like my price. I think you flew all this way for nothing." Esteban drags the tip of my switchblade up my stomach, trailing a fine line of Pablo's blood on my stomach.

"I've reconsidered. We have a deal," Victor says.

A smile creases Esteban's face. "*Muy bien!* You will not be disappointed." Then he looks at me and his smile broadens. "So now I finish my other business."

My heart is beating so hard that my vision blurs. Only the knife stays in focus.

"I'll take her too," I hear Victor say.

"She's not part of the deal."

"She is now. Take it or leave it."

Esteban places the switchblade against my throat. "Her pulse moves the blade," he laughs. "A sure sign of guilt."

"Do we have a deal or not?"

Esteban sighs. The blade clicks back into its handle. "We have a deal."

July 29, 1986, 11:39 P.M.

"It all fell into place just liked you wanted."

The sirens are getting closer. Jack grabs my hand and pulls me down the hallway toward the back door. "I parked on the other block. We can cut through the ally."

He puts his arm around me and helps me along. The long end of the cuff slaps against my knee.

Time flashes by in frames. I see Jack's car. Then his face flickering in the street lights. The door of the Last Call. My Ducatti on its stand. Then to the top of the stairs leading down to his bedroom.

"We need to get that cuff off. Then I think we need to get the hell out of town."

"Where were you…?" I ask. "All that time?"

"Zhukov's men were all around the house. As soon as they left, then Larry came in."

"Did you see Carmen?"

He drops his eyes. "Yes."

I step away from the stairs. "And she's down there? Waiting?"

"Reno—"

"Answer me."

"I was coming up to the house after I heard the gunshots, and she ran right into me."

I should have known. I turn away from him and head for the front door.

"Reno. I asked her what the hell was going on. I still don't know what happened."

I whirl around. "She told me that it was all your idea, Jack. Your plan, your way, that you were only using me. Which is true. It all fell into place just liked you wanted. Carmen's free, the Russians are off your back, and their new man gets to rape my corpse."

He looks at me evenly, his eyes clear. "She asked me to go with her. To make a choice. So I did, Reno, and I chose you. I chose us. That's what I always wanted, no matter what you think." He rubs his eyes. "So look, you have a choice too. You can trust me, go down these stairs, I'll cut off those damn cuffs and we'll go someplace, any place. Or you can walk out of here, beaten half to death, trailing a handcuff—and what? Try to make it to Victor's? Hide somewhere? You can't keep doing this, Reno. It's only a matter of time."

"Where is Carmen now?"

He doesn't answer and I stand there, wondering, like I always do. Wanting to trust him. Wanting to let go of the fear, of the hurt. All of it.

Fuck it.

I turn around and walk back out, heading toward my motorcycle.

"Reno! Wait, damn it!" Jack yells after me.

I ignore Jack and keep moving toward the door. The cold steel of the cuffs bites into my skin. I wrap the loose end around my wrist and up my arm like barbed wire around a post. I kick open the front door and escape into the cool air outside.

"Reno, seriously, where are you going to go?" yells Jack from the doorway of the Last Call.

As I step into the street, I look back and give him the finger. His mouth is open in a wide O.

Out of instinct or luck, I stop.

Just as a car flies by, its horn blaring a second later.

I see its tail lights disappear down the road. Jack shakes his head.

I cross the street, start the Ducatti with a roar and rocket down the street.

The wind rushes over me with a whispered hush as I spilot the motorcycle through the darkness.

I don't need anyone.

Fuck them all.

Printed in the United States
By Bookmasters